How to Tie Your Shoes

T0152314

Nikola Petković

HOW TO TIE YOUR SHOES

Translated from the Croatian by Nikola Petković

DALKEY ARCHIVE PRESS

Originally published by Algoritam as *Kako svezati cipele* in 2011.

Copyright © 2011 by Nikola Petković
Translation copyright © 2017 by Nikola Petković
First Dalkey Archive edition, 2017.

Library of Congress Cataloging-in-Publication Data
Names: Petković, Nikola, 1962- author, translator.
Title: How to tie your shoes / Nikola Petkovic.
Other titles: Kako svezati cipele. English
Description: First edition. | Victoria, TX : Dalkey Archive Press, 2017.
Identifiers: LCCN 2016049405 | ISBN 9781628971736 (pbk. : acid-free paper)
Subjects: LCSH: Fathers and sons--Fiction. | Psychic trauma--Fiction. | Croatia--
History--1990---Fiction.
Classification: LCC PG1619.26.E78 K3513 2017 | DDC 891.8/235--dc23
LC record available at https://lccn.loc.gov/2016049405

www.dalkeyarchive.com
Victoria, TX / McLean, IL / Dublin

Dalkey Archive Press publications are, in part, made possible through
the support of the University of Houston-Victoria and its programs in
creative writing, publishing, and translation.

Printed on permanent/durable acid-free paper

To Nedo, Vasko, Robi, File and Tin

This book would not be possible without the support and encouragement of my family and friends. I want to thank to all of them. I am especially grateful to the first reader of this manuscript, my friend Andrea, and the last reader, my spouse Jasna. Its English version, the first draft of which was completed during my residential stay at Hald Hovengaard near Viborg in Denmark, would never have acquired its final shape without my editor, Nathan Redman, whose patience and collegiality were constant encouragement throughout my travels through my, I hope, second language.

How to Tie Your Shoes

I

1.
Dad's going to die. Soon. My brother and I are standing beside his hospital bed.

I've never been sick, he says. *I used to come here to see those who are sick. Now I'm here, alone, all by myself . . . only, and with you . . . and you don't need me anymore. You're both grown up now.*

2.

Indeed we are. We grew up. My brother's thirty-six. He works with computers. Some weird sub-specialization, he told me. There are only three of them who do this stuff in the entire country. He studied psychology and he dropped it. I have no idea whether he replaced it with anything else. Other than computers. Perhaps he never cared for it to begin with. We seldom talk. Except for the moments when fathers die. He's married and has a son. I'm forty-five. I'm a university professor. Unlike my brother, I never had the courage to quit anything. I have a son too. I'm also married. We're the grown-ups. Big boys. Tall. Dad's not tall anymore. He's rather long now.

There are three bags hanging by his bed:

One is full of blood.

One is full of urine.

One is full of nothing.

Once he dies, I'll place him inside this third, empty one.

3.

I don't like it when they shove people inside caskets. I told my wife the other day to burn me and scatter my ashes at sea. I told her to do it together with our son, Tin. I hope he'll be a grown-up by then. A big boy. Strong. You see, those urns can be heavy. It depends on how much of the ash they collect for you and give you to take home. It's common knowledge they don't give you all of it. I believe they do burn the entire body, but for some reason they dump the majority of the ash. But even the little you get is still way too heavy to carry. Tin is male, so he can hold the urn properly. He can help his mom. They should do it while they're on the boat. On a calm, windless day. Windless is important because of the ashes. That shit can blind you if it hits you in the eyes. I know exactly where I want to be scattered and, before the time comes, I'll let them know that too. This will be "The Place"—my Salt Lake.

4.

I'm claustrophobic and I would suffocate sealed inside a raw wooden casket. Although, it would be unfair of me not to tell you that I've had plenty of chances to see some beautiful caskets. Even those sponsored by the Church. I saw one, for instance, with an engraving of the entire Last Supper squad. All the Apostles, Jesus, Judas . . . like a modest, old-fashioned soccer team . . . what was it? Was it Bayern Munich? Was it '72, '74, or '76? The year we kicked the Krauts' asses. Or was it the German national team that resembled the guys on that casket I saw? I remember a Yugoslavia vs. Germany game. The score was 2-1. I remember they had that Gerd Müller guy—a fantastic player. Man, he could score. His volley was deadly and, what was truly amazing about him, he needed almost no space around him to nail the ball. These were the times when all the soccer players (unlike the Apostles) were short and ugly, meaning real. Not like today when they all look like clones, their hairdos gelled to perfection, their bodies shaved . . . Well, there's always that two-bagger Ribéry who makes you feel good about yourself. Now back to the game. Our goalie back in the '70s was Enver Marić. He stopped Müller's penalty kick. Dad screamed in ecstasy: *this is the real Bosnian, this is my paesano . . . Enver!*

5.

According to one of his stories, Dad is Montenegrin. From the small city of Cetinje. In his other story he claims he's from the Bosnian city of Doboj. All of his stories are true. He grew up in Croatia, in an orphanage, in the large coastal city of Split. This is another true story. Afterward he lived with his mom. They shared a house in a small village. Pridjel. In Bosnia. Back in the '70s he was just Bosnian. The other day, when we were returning from Zagreb, he told me how we, the Petković clan, were actually from Konavle, a village near Dubrovnik. What happened to Korčula, I asked him coldly. I got over my bewilderment about the different versions of our ancestral history long ago. He changed his stories so often that no one in their right mind could bother to follow them, much less to verify their content. To him, they were all true. Thus, they were true to us too.

Fuck it, Son, some of us managed to swim all the way to Korčula. All the way from where, I asked. *Where else do you think they'd swim from? From the Cetina River? Over the mountains of Montenegro . . . dumbass, why did I pay for your education?*
Fuck, man, why didn't he tell me about that Konavle shit back in the '90s, when I could've cashed it in and saved my ass? When war was around the corner, and when all the pure and full-blooded Croats were calling me up in the middle of the night, peering inside my veins, counting my blood cells?

6.

On my way home Dad's words were haunting me. You're both grown up now. Yes, we are. While he was saying that, I was holding his hand. Still, some anger snuck up on me. The same anger I've felt ever since he quit taking care of me. First, when I was a small child and in need of care, and afterward when I didn't need it anymore. What would it have cost him if he'd decided to disappear during this second half of his life: the easier one? In the halftime when I was really a grown-up. Yes, I'm a big boy, but what does he want to tell me? That I don't need him anymore? As if he'd ever been there for me.

My brother's telling me, this whole situation . . . *it's hardest on Mom. She's alone. And she's not used to being alone. Dad's just fine here in the hospital. He has a routine. He's never alone. Somebody's always taking care of him. He has a routine, see. And Mom . . . she's all by herself.*

7.

When, at the beginning of the '90s, just before the war broke out, our brother hung himself, I was in the States. Writing my PhD. Or living in exile. I don't really remember anymore what actually went on back then and in what order it happened. What best describes my situation back then? Was it the task of writing a dissertation or living in exile? A PhD can be a form of exile, too, if someone or something is making you do it. The war was raging back home. And there I was, sitting calmly in the library or at home, in the homes I kept changing, pretending I'd found mine . . . pretending I could remove myself from the tragedy I'd left behind. Alone in the world, limping through a new language, I was trying desperately not to fall behind in a fucked-up competition with American students, who used to look at me with a mixture of empathy, pity, and a total absence of understanding my in-between life . . . and yet, at the same time, never alone with my memories that got so mixed up as time went by. Sometimes I wasn't sure what came first. Was it war, was it my parents' separation, was it the day when I learned that I was part Croatian, part Bosnian, part Serb, and the rest of me Montenegrin . . . Don't forget, my dad's "true" stories kept changing. Mom and Dad divorced when I was seven. That I knew for certain and it never changed. Dad left without a word. Mom stayed without a word. I was looking for words until I turned sixteen. Then, I started to write poetry. If you know how to do it, you don't really need to search for words in order to write a decent poem. And to write poetry when you're sixteen isn't strange at all. Back then, in the '70s, all the sixteen year olds around me were writing poetry. I continued doing it all my life. I'm even doing it now when, as Dad put it, I'm a grown-up. A mature man writing poetry, well, that is strange.

8.

Our stepbrother killed himself at his home in Rijeka. After I found out, I ran into the water at Belmar beach in New Jersey. The phone rang at my friend's place. She was the sister of a poet I went to school with. He taught me to eat butter with every meal. He got me addicted to it—a slice of hot white bread and ice-cold butter with every single meal. Even with chili sprinkled on top. We met in Austin, in a hole-in-the-wall called "Texas Showdown" on Guadalupe Street. When I was on vacation, visiting my family, he called me up in Croatia and told me to come to Belmar to stay with his family. On our way back to the States, we sailed from Rijeka to Red Hook, Brooklyn. The war was going on in Croatia and we were smuggling peanuts. One-way: Brooklyn to Rijeka. Not even the code name "peanuts" could have saved those same peanuts from being the means and the fabric used to stop people's lives. The peanut-users were killing people to defend themselves from others—from those whose lives were on the other side of the border—the border that wasn't supposed to be moved. Those to whom we were delivering peanuts, who were arguing with those others—those across the border, were explaining that our borders are natural. Yes, our president, a psycho who identified himself with Franco and publicly bragged, I'm so delighted that my wife is neither Serb nor Jew, claimed that Croatia had its natural borders. Go figure! The war was out of control, and the only reason for the fight was that both sides divided by the border had the exact same convictions. Both sides imagined their borders to be natural. Now, when we were heading back to the States, no one mentioned the cargo anymore. The entire vessel was somehow lighter and we were sailing much faster.

Nikola's not here, my friend's sister said, answering the phone the day my stepbrother killed himself. The neighbors found him hanging in his living room in downtown Rijeka. *What, what,* the father screamed, what? *Nikola's not here*, she repeated in Croatian. I'd written down a few phrases in green marker on the whiteboard above the phone, in case of emergency. Just in case something goes wrong back home. In case someone hangs himself, if someone's house is destroyed . . . I wrote down a few phrases just in case. Some of them relating to natural disasters, others to man-made disasters. *He's not there, he's not there . . .* my father kept screaming across the ocean. And after I learned about my stepbrother's death, after she told me that my dad was screaming and, at the same time, it seemed to her, choking back tears, I ran down to the beach alone. I wanted to swim, to swim endlessly in the salty sea.

9.

She told me they called me. I told her my stepbrother killed himself. My grandmother was the first to tell me. I was sitting on a boardwalk fence in Belmar. My grandmother knew how to fly. She flew from one sea to another sea, across the oceans. She did it the same fast and invisible way she managed to escape from the concentration camp back in 1943 somewhere in northern Italy. Some place called Gonars. Near Monfalcone. Despite wearing high heels, the only pair of shoes she was allowed to take when the soldiers stormed our house and took her to the camp, she moved fast. See, here she is today. In Belmar. Dressed in a short white raincoat. The same one she wore on her way to detention. She came to tell me that my stepbrother had hung himself. And this is what I'm now telling Katie, for whom I wrote all the emergency instructions on a whiteboard above the phone. And I told her I was going back. I wanted to be at the funeral. *No*, she said, *there's a war going on there. I don't give a flying fuck,* I said. There's a war going on here too, but it hasn't officially been announced. Back home at least it has. It's been announced more than once. Never officially. Maybe that's the reason why only those who are directly affected by it take that war for a war. After all, we Central Europeans are a culture bound by protocols, thriving on controlled chaos. Therefore, to make something official, we must always stamp it. God forbid one should trust somebody's word. It all has to be written down and stamped. Never just uttered.

In the end, I didn't go. Dad told me not to. *People are dying here*, he said when we finally got to talk to each other across the sea. *I can't afford to lose another one of you guys.*

10.

When I came back home, my brother's mother told me: *it's your brother who's now suffering the most*. In the beginning there were three of us. My father brought me into his new marriage. His wife brought her son into the new marriage. And the two of them made their own son. Now, there are just two of us left. The oldest one is dead. I am undone by exile, angry at being abandoned, and the youngest one—the only one among us whose family didn't fall apart . . . he who managed to escape all the advances death has made to him, who is untouched by separation and safely lives with his mom and dad . . . he suddenly got the harshest part of the entire family gig. How come? Easy. He's her son, and he's my father's son too. I'm only my father's son. Not her son. He, the dead one, he was her son. Not my father's. And now is it toughest on my brother who lives with both of his parents? I hope not because he has to deal with one death and one displacement. Maybe I'm asking too much. Maybe it's the way it is just because life is the way it is . . .

11.

And now he's returning her favor. Saying, it's hardest on my mom. *No*, I told him, looking him straight in his eyes. *This time it's Dad who's suffering the most. He's ill. Unlike the rest of us, your mom included, he's aware of the nearness of death. He almost knows his own expiration date.* We don't know jack shit about ours, for the moment. He too doesn't know exactly how and when . . . but he knows it's close.

12.

My brother is silent. Is he afraid he'd make me angry enough to finally start talking in front of our father? To tell him my story. My true story about our lives. How come he doesn't know that opening up in front of our dad is something I don't know how to do? I have no clue how to talk in front of my father. Does he realize that my whole life I've wanted to speak out about the dignity and sacredness of life, but that, for the life of me, I couldn't open my mouth in front of my father? What's he afraid of now? Of my own fear? If so, then can he differentiate it from his own fear? He should, because it seems to me that he's the grown-up out of us two. Three, if you count the dead one. Perhaps because he's the only one who remained in one piece? The only one who, in fact, didn't fall apart. Or maybe it's simpler than that. Maybe he's covering for the mother who is covering for him. Are they protecting each other from the world? From the father whose death is entering the path of their love—the love between a mother and a son? And if what I see is in fact what is really to be seen, if this is the truth, then it seems that the two of them are indeed suffering the most.

I don't know whether this is the truth. I have no idea whether my words are hitting the truth at all. I don't know what the truth is anyway. How can I know it this time? Everything I'm telling you, this whole story is a story of my reality. To me it's a true story. My story. I'm not angry at a single bit of it. Everything I'm telling you is mine. Including the story. And only mine. Anyone who might get angry at it would be angry with me. Not angry with what I'm talking about. Angry with me, regardless of what I say. Angry whether I told it or not. And I won't allow anyone to be angry at my truth. Why? Because I don't expect it to become anyone else's truth.

13.

I'm looking at my dad. He's playing with his watch, putting it on and taking it off his wrist. He had surgery. The doctor told me that they managed to remove the primary cancer, and that, as far as he was concerned, everything was OK. *And what doesn't concern you*, I ask. *Well, that's not OK.* But that, he tells me, is not his domain.

Therefore, it means that my dad will die in someone else's domain. He will die some other death that is, by default, unknown to the doctor who operated on him.

14.
The Patriarch is sitting at the head of the table. Talking. He's telling us how, once he gets better, he'll go to the village in the woods, to the home of a friend who has a dog. And how he'll live there in that village, alone in his friend's house with his friend's dog. *Where will your friend go while you're in that house with his dog*, I ask.

15.

My dad informs us that he'll take care of his chemotherapy all by himself. He'll make all the arrangements with the nurse. He'll make the appointments. He knows we're busy enough without having to take care of his appointments. He knows that we have our own things to worry about. We're not small kids anymore, he knows. Remember, we're the grown-ups. The image of the-Patriarch-sitting-at-the-head-of-the-table-in-the-dining-room comes back to my mind too. Just now. The Patriarch who daydreams of a dog, of a friend, of a village . . . of a dog he doesn't have, of a friend he doesn't have, of a village that is not there anymore. Well, I'm not too sure about the friend. Perhaps he exists, but for the moment he has no name. But that village, see, that village has its name. It must be his village in Bosnia—the village he left long ago, along with the Boy Scouts on their weeklong trip to the Adriatic coast that became his second home. He never went back to his village. Is he himself that friend of his he wants to visit in the village that got tired of waiting for him to return?

16.

He's sitting at the dining table. He can't stop sitting at the dining table. He keeps talking. He talks without the proper pause one needs in order to take a breath between words . . . He's the main character of his endless monologues . . . himself, himself, and only himself . . . everything he says is about himself . . . everything the others say is about him. He displays his boundless ego . . . Yes, once again he's the center of our undivided attention! We sit around the table poker-faced, pretending to focus on his talk. Like wax statues in some demented family museum, pretending to be totally tuned in. This is nothing new to us. This is how it's always been. And this is how it is now. And this is how it will be until he dies—until his world, solely made of him, containing only him, expels him.

Where was I in all this? Dad was that huge, heavy curtain dividing my space from the entirety of the world. Well, it used to be even worse. Before he turned into a curtain, he used to be a wall—an impenetrable one. In order to soften him until he turned into a curtain, I slowly undressed him, peeling away all the layers of the fabric he was made of. And I saw that he was made of thick gray bricks. I dismantled that wall, brick by brick. In doing so, I felt like those pardoned Stasi spies that were forced to tear down the Berlin Wall with their bare hands. And once the wall was gone, what did they see? The same stuff I see today when our wall suddenly perished. They saw themselves in the mirror along with the cheap clay and the cardboard the wall was in fact made of all these years while everyone believed in its firmness and timeless might.

He won't give up talking. In a little while, he won't be able to sit anymore. He'll give up sitting. But he'll continue to talk. Then, tired of sitting, he'll lie down. He won't give up talking. He won't give up talking until he's still, until he stops gasping for air.

17.
Once he shuts up, I'll sneak into his bed and start talking like a madman. I'll monitor his breathing like a machine that counts breaths—first in-breaths and then out-breaths. And I'll remind myself of the medical fact: the dying can still hear you. *Watch out what you talk about when you're around the dying*, doctors say. *Hearing is the last sense to go.*

How do they know that, when everything they touch, in the end, dies? And that statement about the ears . . . it hurts. We know nothing about the timetable of the dying ears. It hurts especially if those ears belong to someone who is close to you. I can remember my father's ears quite well. They were small, darkish, and hairy. Elegantly stuck on to the sides of his head, they didn't draw attention. Their hairiness did. The hair in them looked like charred bonsai trees.

Again, how do doctors know that about the ears being the last organ to die? Is there an ear domain they specialize in? Or perhaps death itself tells them its ear secret? Doctors like to know. I know that. I live with an MD. Doctors pretend to know. I know that too. I married an MD. We have parties to which doctors come. They drink and talk about everything they know. And they know it all . . . Fuck them and their ear fixation. I'll sneak in underneath my father's sheet whether they like it or not. And I'll talk and talk and talk until the last breath leaves his body. I'll tell him everything I ever wanted to tell him, everything I could have ever told him. Everything I needed to tell him . . . I'll tell him everything I was obliged to tell him as a son but never had the guts to do. I'll spit out all the stuff I stored up over the years of getting tired of not being heard. I'll tell him everything that came to me after I lost the last hope that even repeating the same words, warnings, wonders . . . could have any effect on him. Simply put, I'll talk until he finally kicks the bucket. Until he drops dead, killed by my words, by my remarks that, just like a proctologist who pokes his finger into every hole, I will shovel deep inside his dead ears. And if his ears hear me, great. If they don't, it's all right too. I'm used to it.

18.
Yes, Dad, I can give you my book. This time, under my conditions.
I can do it the same way you used to give me gifts, letting me hold
them for a day and then taking them back to your place. Remember
the small radio, and the camera, Dad? An old camera from the
times they used to keep those devices in leather cases. Wait, this is
how it was: I used to come to your place and you would proudly
open the leather case to show me the dedication written inside it.
To Niko for his . . . I don't know which birthday in a row. Then,
you would just shut that leather case and put the gift back on the
shelf. It was supposed to be my present but I wasn't allowed to
take it with me. You used to tell me I wasn't big enough to handle
such expensive presents. You told me to wait. The time was never
right. And I waited. And I still wait. I remember . . . it was my
birthday. Actually there were two of my birthdays in a row. First I
was nine and then I was ten. And for both of these birthdays you
gave me a book. Books I could take. One was about the marvels
of the world such as pyramids, the Grand Canyon, the Hagia
Sophia . . . those four heads the Americans used to destroy a
mountain with somewhere in South Dakota . . . while the other
one was about the advantages of living under the rule of president
Tito. Both glamorous. Well, the other one a little more so. Tito was
bigger than the Taj Mahal. Older than Machu Picchu. We knew
that. The book had pictures with Tito and tigers given to him by
the emperor Haile Selassie, with Sophia Loren, J. F. Kennedy . . .
him sailing the globe on his famous ship The Seagull on many of
his peace missions. Tito loved smoking Cuban cigars and allegedly
drank impressive amounts of whiskey. The cigars were Castro's and
the whiskey was Carter's.

Back to my birthdays. In both of those books, on both of their front
pages, you wrote the following: To Niko for his 10th birthday. In
both cases you decided to change the rules. I was allowed to take
these books home. Was I allowed to do that two years in a row
because, in both cases, I didn't need to wait for the right time to
walk away with them, or were they not as precious as cameras and
radios? Or did you find a way to stop time? Was I really ten for

two consecutive years, and those books were somehow aware of that? Even today I don't know whether you gave me another year of life or whether you took one away from me. Today it doesn't matter. What matters is: that was the moment when you and I ran out of time!

Here is how we'll go about it. Instead of giving you my book, I'll write you into existence, and I'll give you to everyone who wants to take you home. You'll be made up of letters. But there's a small requirement that all of those who want to take you away from me would need to fulfill: in order to take you with them they must assure me that time will stop.

19.
We don't believe in God. We write it with a capital G though. We did it after 1990. Just because this is the way the new people that came into power told the journalists to write it in the newspapers: with a capital G! Between 1945 and 1990 God officially didn't exist within the borders of the Socialist Federal Republic of Yugoslavia. If he was mentioned it was either for the purpose of cursing, or as proof that in the outside world there existed countries that were all backward, superstitious, capitalist, and stupid, misled by the opium for the masses. That was how Marx saw god with a lowercase g. In the early '90s we changed the name of our country. Yugoslavia was divided into smaller units. My leftover bit of Yugoslavia became Croatia. Our new president told us that our thousand-year-old-dream finally became a reality. Most of us were happy and fulfilled. Some of us were perplexed by the idea of the millennial hibernation of our now independent state. We tried to assess the condition of a patient lying in a coma for a thousand years. We weren't too happy imagining his state. Our passports changed color. Their red covers turned blue. They also changed names. They weren't called passports any more. They became homeland-booklets. I know it sounds crazy. It sounds crazy in Croatian too. And god crossed the border and came back with a capital G. We finally achieved our country, got rid of the Serbs, and changed the rules: whatever was prohibited in Yugoslavia was now allowed and vice versa. We became free at last.

As for my family, we don't believe in god. We also don't believe that once you die you go anywhere except into nothingness. And if you turn into nothing, how can you read? Why should you carry books into emptiness? There's nobody there, nothing is there, neither are you there. My dad will go there very soon. Perhaps I can save him somehow, through language—my language? Using my own words—those same words he ran away from his entire life. Maybe I'll write him into existence and give him to those who read. I must devise a plan.

20.

I called my dad today. He hasn't taken a shit in four days, he said, and then he added that he called his daughter-in-law who told him that she'd found him a doctor, and after that he filled up the entire bowl. What, you shat because she found you a doctor?

No, because of the mineral water the doctor recommended.
Take some magnesium, I said, *with a glass of water. It tastes better and makes you shit. No*, he said, *the mineral water is good enough. You shit like a seagull after you take it; I'm living proof of it. And by the way, magnesium is dangerous.*
But people your age, I was persistent, *even healthier than you, take magnesium. It's totally safe. My father-in-law takes it every day.*

No! He's stubborn. He says his daughter-in-law found him a doctor. But he has a doctor. The doctor is his other daughter-in-law. She's my wife. *No!* The other daughter-in-law found him the doctor. His younger son's wife.

Dad doesn't want me to help him. In comparison with death, I'm a burden.

21.

That burden thing shouldn't be the problem. Maybe I'm overreacting. I know that, by now, I should have learned to forgive. I should simply tell myself, who cares anymore. What happened, happened and is behind us. What do I care who is whose doctor anymore, and who is whose son? I remember the story when my grandpa went to Zagreb to learn how to become a barber. When he arrived there, his aunt bought him his first pair of shoes. His father was a shoemaker and my grandpa arrived in Zagreb in a pair of slippers. Then his aunt, I told you that already, bought him a pair of shoes. And his father was a shoemaker. Got the point?

22.

Father came home. I went to visit him. I took a deep breath while waiting for his wife to slide the gate open. It was my first time in their new place. Now, when the countdown started, I can finally see where they live. When I visited him the last time he lived in a residential neighborhood in the upper town. A rather secluded outpost that he actually called a village. It was easier for him that way. He never learned the rules of the city. Not even in the case with a city, and this definitely is the case with Rijeka, that had no rules to begin with. When all the rules are tamed, domesticated, internalized, localized, softened, democratic, ecumenical, crypto-fascist, isolationist, all-inclusive, Nazi-proletarian, Catholic . . . all that put together in a local melting pot. My father brought his village into the city he chose to live in. And that portable village of his had no room to grow in the city. But it kept on growing anyway. It grew bigger and bigger until it boomed out of all proportion. Suddenly, no place was left in the city where either my father or his village could settle. Frankly speaking, in a city there is neither and nor should there be any place left for a village to inhabit. But why does it have the need to grow after its voluntary displacement? A city is a city. A village is a village. Once brought into the city, even if it's placed in the heart of its bearer, even if it's no bigger than the size of one's own personal symbol, no matter how hard it tries, a village has no place for growth. It even has no place to properly expand. It's not even possible to worship it; neither as something imagined nor as something real. When things become available to us, they somehow stop being real. Daily routine produces boredom. Things become real to us only in the eyes of memory. They start living fully once they're gone, wandering alone way out of our reach. It's impossible to take the sounds of the village and use them to undermine the asphalt of the city. Except in our memory. And unless memory contains a piece of farmland, the memory of a peasant can't be fulfilled. After their own memories first reject and then abandon them, peasants are gradually turned into losers. The sense of loss, together with the unawareness of the power of memory, turns those peasants with their portable villages into plain tyrants. A village, the same village they left in order to come to the city to give us a better life, can't live here. No! And it was history, which like my father almost always serves its own interests, that placed him in the city. And it was here, in the city, with the very intention of my father's portable village cohabiting with the urban surroundings, that he died. Having no space for a Big Bang, the village imploded. Unlike in history, its implosion left the city walls untouched. It didn't even scratch a single façade. The entire yard fence remained intact. The rubber boots of the Patriarch could do nothing to the hated asphalt no matter how hard he marched around the suburbs. The city resisted the explosion. Those who exploded were all of us inside our house—the family.

Fuck me dead if the city, not my father, is to blame for all the shit. Because the curse of the city explains the fact that I didn't know where my father lived. Until his intestines started to rot. Until his own blood abandoned him without warning. The blood that, for months and months, unnoticed, kept slowly draining, leaving small spots on the cold ceramic toilet bowl, screaming its warning, the same blood that runs partly through my veins, the blood that, month after month, coursed through me, filling me with the question: where did your father move to?

23.

He sits in the apartment the two of them bought together to make their lives easier, and for those in the family who were in need. Before they did it they sold their big house in the suburbs. We're helping everyone but us, was their mantra. But there was another group of us included. Us who knew how to take care of ourselves by ourselves alone. I wasn't a part of that in-need-of category. They didn't want to bother me with their help. Everything's so easy for Niko, my father's wife used to say, he's smart and he'll find ways to take care of himself. And that's exactly what I did. Liberated from my father's care ever since I was seven, along the way, I found the means to take care of myself. I started doing it the moment my father, driving a small white Fiat 750, first in reverse and then straight downhill, left me. It was then when his help, which I needed so much, disappeared. And being left alone made me strong. I took care of myself. Partly not to be in their way, not to bother them. And partly to see whether his wife's prophecy—the prophecy of a woman who, along with a bee sting (completely unknown to me) on my chin (completely known to me) entered a family that was mine as well—the prediction about me being a smart boy who would succeed without them in life, and who would come through. And it all fell into place. See, I'm doing fine. So fine that I don't even need to know my father's home address. The address in my own city—in the city where, always thinking of helping others, my father moved so many times.

24.

Doctor D. called. My wife, Jasna, met him while at work. She told him my father was in the hospital. *Have Niko call me*, he said. I did it immediately. Together, we arranged the chemotherapy schedule. The target organ is my dad's liver. It was there where the cancer, defeated by the success achieved in the first doctor's domain, decided to hide. Inside the safe haven of dad's liver. Inside that other domain that is completely unknown to the surgeon who operated on my father. It's there where the cancer decided to move.

25.

Saturday morning. We stopped by my dad's house. It was the first time Tin and Jasna visited their new place. Dad's wife is showing me the cellar. To me, it looks like a crypt. I'm indifferent. Dad's saying he feels it won't end well. He said he called the hospital and made an appointment for chemo. I tell him not to do anything without telling me, because I made all the arrangements with the doctors, and I'm in charge. *No*, he insists, *you only know the doctors, and they can't do anything about the appointments. I know the nurses. They make the schedule.* Without telling the doctors . . . I wonder but, as usual, I'm silent. But I will tell him this, too, once I sneak in inside his ear. *Yes*, he says, *the nurses do it all.* Jasna doesn't agree. She's telling him that he's wrong. She's an MD. But she married me, and the fact that she married me, in my father's eyes, makes her not so good at recalling a patient's medical history. And if she's not so good at recalling a patient's medical history, how can she be good at making a diagnosis? And if she can't make a proper diagnosis, then how can she prescribe a therapy of any use? If you follow the line of his argument, you can foresee its cataclysmic consequences. I take time to remind him that I was the one who arranged the surgery, finding the best possible surgeon to operate on him. He repeats how the nurse was the one who arranged everything, surgery included. Jasna's telling him that he's just plain wrong about it. She says, *it was he, Niko who did it.* And he listens without a slight sign of disagreement. While he's talking to her, he doesn't look at me at all. He simply can't accept my help. He can't accept that he's not the one who's in charge. And it was he who, lying in the hospital bed, told me I was a grown-up.

26.

It's Monday morning. I call my father. I tell him that, next week, we must see Doctor D. He's a gastroenterologist. He'll take a look at him, I say. He'll examine him together with his colleague, the oncologist. *Thank you*, he says. It seems to be easier for him to communicate with me when he doesn't see me, when he can replace me with a receiver. I tell him there's no need to thank me. *Don't worry*, I add. *We can keep it all under control, I promise, we'll keep it all under control. As for everything else*, I say . . . *we're in it together, regardless of what happens, Dad.*

27.

A week's gone by. *Where are you,* my father asks. *I'm on my way to pick up some visiting Chinese writers,* I answer. *First I'm going to get Tin from kindergarten and afterward the two of us will pick up the Chinese writers.* The Chinese visitors are at lunch now in a suburb of Rijeka—Trsat. There, where my father had a house before he sold it. Less than a kilometer from it, near the city soccer stadium. The Chinese are visiting us. More precisely, the Chinese writers are returning to visit the Croatian writers. Not too long ago, four of us, all writers, visited China. I remember the three of us taking a stroll in downtown Shanghai, pimps swarming all around us. They were so annoying. We couldn't finish a sentence without being cornered by pimps. *Come on, fucky-fucky, sucky-sucky, nice women, pussy-pussy, I make you a good plice, good plice . . .*

What happened to fuckin' r, I wondered. *Good plice, good plice, pussy tight, small pussy . . .* And when it appeared as though fucking would be mandatory, I thought of the secluded omnipotence of homosexuality and uttered the words that saved us. I looked at the Chinese pussy-vendor, and pointed first at the president of the Croatian Writers' Society, who, not only among the Chinese, but in general, looked like a bigfoot, and then to the famous dramatist who, in fact, was the size of almost every other Chinese in the square. And then I started, *this is how it is, the small one here, he's my bitch, and this fuckin' giant, see how big he is, well he's buttfucking me . . . and we're so happy, nice ass, nice ass, fucky-fucky, happy-fucky . . .* It made the pimp disappear in a jiffy. Not only that. It turned out that that fuckin' guy had high-speed intranet and broadcast the information instantaneously. Being linked to all the other pimps in Shanghai, he signaled that we were of no use to them. My little treatise on faggotry made all the pimps vanish for the rest of the night.

I wondered if I should tell this story to my dad over the phone. Would it be appropriate? He started telling me the story he's told me a zillion times, as usual, assuming that I'd never heard it before. The story about the Japanese sake-makers he hosted when he was the head of the Yugoslavian national winery. It's not as though I haven't heard that story over and over, memorized all its versions too. *Everyone has his delegation*, I jump in, in the middle of his story, *I had my Japanese, and Tin now has his Chinese* . . .

When I was Tin's age, perhaps a year older, Dad drove the Japanese officials along the coast. They were visiting Rijeka. The official name for a visit of that kind was "The Delegation." In theory it meant a group of people, usually from abroad, coming to investigate possible business opportunities in the Socialist Federal Republic of Yugoslavia. In reality, The Delegation meant a group of people, no less than four and no more than six, that, on the pretext of coming to do something of tremendous importance on both a national and an international level, accompanied by domestic politicians, just came here to eat, drink, and fuck. I remember that the Japanese delegation supplemented the triad of pleasure by puking as well. Actually, I've never since seen anyone as good at puking as the Japanese. The way they vomit . . . After seeing them throw up, their faces gray, their eyes popping out of their sockets . . . I figured out there must have been something immensely wrong with that entire concept of The Delegation. Having had that experience, despite being a kid, the word "delegation" sounded to me way more sinister than the strange word "Japanese" did to a kid my age.

The story Dad is repeating to infinity goes something like this: somewhere on the island of Krk, our car slowed down. We were driving behind a man riding a donkey. And I wouldn't allow the driver to overtake him because I wanted to look at the donkey.

Being a city boy, it was the first encounter with a domestic animal of any kind for me. And that donkey was so cute, calm, and, unfortunately too slow for The Delegation. And I didn't want to stop staring at the donkey. Or, to be honest, it wasn't the entire donkey that fascinated me. It was just its ass. You must understand me. They were the first three unusual things that I'd seen up to that point in my then short life: the Japanese, The Delegation, and a donkey—too much to take in even for a grown-up, too much excitement. When the driver finally overtook the donkey-rider, I started to cry. And supposedly (and this is my father's version), I wouldn't stop crying for hours . . .

I was sobbing: *Why did you overtake him, why, you shouldn't have done it* . . . all I wanted was to just stare at the donkey.

If father's addition to my memory is correct, I'm not so sure what the better choice for the Japanese would have been: to continue peering at the donkey's ass or to listen to my screaming. Be that as it may, it must have been pure Zen, although perhaps a negative one.

Dad and I continue to talk over the phone, remembering delegations and speaking about the past and the present. And being a father myself, driving the Chinese with my son in the car, I repeatedly wonder whether to tell the Shanghai story to my dad, just to make him laugh. Even though our conversation flows miraculously smoothly, somehow I have no guts to tell my cunts & pimps fable to my father. On my way to the small picturesque coastal town of Bakar, less than ten kilometers away from Rijeka, I find myself driving behind a truck full of incredibly large rocks. In fact, they look like two gigantic round rocks freshly plucked from the soil. And that truck is driving below twenty kilometers per hour. We're crawling behind it. The moment I get the chance, I pull out and overtake it. In my car, filled with Chinese writers, my son Tin starts to cry: *Why did you overtake him, why, you shouldn't have done it* . . . *all I wanted was to just stare at the rocks.*

28.

Tin doesn't know that Dad is dying. He knows that Grandpa died. *Grandpa died*, he tells me, *and now he's in a graveyard. I love him; I love him because he's in a graveyard. Will he be back*, Tin asks. *No*, I say. *Nobody returns from a cemetery. How come no one returns*, says Tin, *you and Mom always return from a cemetery. Yes, we do, but we're not inside. We're not in the soil. Huh*, says Tin, *then it means that Grandpa's in the earth. Well. Just have him get up, leave the cemetery, and come back. He can't*, I answer. *He can't because he died*, says Tin. *Yes*, I confirm. *He must be somewhere else now, in some other world*, Tin continues to talk. *Remember*, I ask him, *the night he was watching us from that star? From the star you said was called "El caballero de triste figura?" No*, answers Tin. We're lying in bed, trying to tuck each other in. We just returned from Dad's place. Today he was pale. When we were leaving, he was able to get up and walk us to the gate.

29.

Grandpa isn't somewhere else, Tin explains; *he went into nothingness. Where did he go*, I ask in amazement. *Into nothingness*, Tin repeats. *Grandpa is nowhere. Remember*, says Tin, *when we were sitting in the church and Grandpa came, he hugged me and told me he was going into nothingness . . . he hugged me first and then he told me that, remember . . . I told you that, Dad . . .*

I don't go to church. I don't believe in god. I avoid churches unless I have to go . . . weddings, funerals, and things like that . . . I was never in church with Tin. This never took place. My wife goes to church sometimes. She believes. Sometimes, on holidays, or when she feels like going, she goes. *When did it happen*, I was perplexed. *In that church, Dad . . . we were together. He hugged us and left. Where, to the graveyard*, I ask. *Yes, into nothingness*, Tin repeats.

30.

He's an artist, a poet, a university professor, scholar, our columnist . . . he writes for the well-known daily paper, he got his PhD in the United States . . . and this is his father, Doctor D. explains to his colleague. He helps me all the time. He possesses a unique dimension of goodness—goodness truly hard to find. Aside from this, he's in power. He's the head of the clinic; an internationally renowned and respected gastroenterologist and a friend of mine. When his goodness and power are in accord with the two seemingly opposed things, with the unexplainable that resides outside ourselves and with the predictable that lives inside us, he can and wants to save a life. He uses all these big words to introduce me to the doctor who later, while in her office, tells me that the border of the civilized western world is the bridge that divides our city. Until 1943, before the capitulation of then Fascist Italy, Rijeka was a story of two cities. Its eastern part was Croatian and its name was Sušak, while its western part was Italian and was called Fiume. After the Partisans liberated the country from the Nazis and other scum, the two cities became one city—the city of Rijeka. Rijeka actually is the same as Fiume and il fiume simply means the river. So the place of division, the river, remained the name of the city. A border in flux became the fixed territory. *What side of the border do you have in mind,* I ask the doctor. She has an ID card with her name and photo pinned to her left breast pocket. In the photo her hair is straight while in reality it is curly. In both cases, it is bleached.

31.

Unlike our professor (Doctor D.), *I see things the way they are, and they're bleak*, she continues. A nurse brings in some coffee. She has an ID card with her name and photo pinned to her left breast. In the photo her hair is curly while in reality it is straight. Is it some kind of conspiracy? Does it say something about the equation of Jupiter with Iovus? Did they swap IDs? Do they have a habit of doing so on occasion? What if this one with the coffee isn't a nurse and the other one isn't a doctor? The faces on their IDs don't match with their faces in reality. The doctor talks about everything except medicine and healing. The nurse remains silent, so I can't grasp the contents of her mind. The conversation goes on about how the people here are stupid, especially those who block up hearths, and how all the young people should pack up and go to the States. The one with curly hair talks of different modes of being civilized, and tells the story of how her mother saw a barefoot person for the first time in her life when she crossed that damned bridge, that bulwark of a civilized world. Yet another of our quasi *familienfuge* made up in a city where, in fact, hardly anyone knows who he is and, speaking of family lines, where exactly he comes from. The fact that they don't have an answer to either of those two questions doesn't prevent them from knowing who they aren't. And they know only too well all the places they're definitely not from. The more ambitious among them, like her husband, whom she speaks about with so much love and admiration for his intellect, not only know who they are but also know what they want to become. He's on his way to Congo, I just learned. You should also go to Congo, the doctor tells me. *You're too smart to stay in Croatia. Actually, you returned to Croatia after living almost half of your adult life in the States . . . you mustn't be that smart after all.*

32.

The doctor talks about her colleagues. She's very opinionated. The doctor talks about philosophy (which is my domain). She finds it incredible that, being a Taurus with a moon in Leo, I became an artist . . . because Leo/Taurus is her exact astrological scheme and she isn't an artist. She talks about everything except possible treatments, my father's chances of survival, a possible cure . . . Dad sits beside me, speechless. I feel uneasy because nobody's talking to him. And I know that he would like to hear a word or two about his illness. Like, how he's doing, what his chances of survival are, how things stand now, and how they will be later. He's never been put in a situation like this before: cancer in an advanced stage that spread to his liver and decimated it. But he's not the topic. The topics are zodiac signs and myself. I'm her husband's age, she repeats. I try to make a joke. I'm thinking of what she had to say about Doctor D. and, to his defense, I state how his optimism is an important ingredient of our generation. Some sort of mutuality is woven into the fabric of our lives: our incurable optimism. Blinding optimism occurs in times when there is nothing else to see. And ours is the generation whose dignity and lives were threatened with annihilation by two seemingly opposite political systems: first by the communists, who came at us in the name of class, and then by the nationalists, who were at our throats in the name of the nation. And what if optimism was the force that made us survive both perils, and kept us not only alive but also occasionally happy? Of course, it amused us within the parameters of a sustainable growth of life and happiness that any totalitarianism can bear. No, she refuses to give in; she's extremely annoyed by optimism. Knowing that on Monday morning three different concoctions that she herself will choose will start running through my father's veins, I decide to give up. I nod in agreement. Instead of defending optimism I go for the safety of cuteness and social submissiveness.

Actually, when I think about it, you're right. Do you know the difference between an optimist and a pessimist, I ask. You mean the one about the two glasses, one half empty and one half full, she replies.

No, not that one, I said, *a pessimist is, in fact, an optimist who is better informed.*

33.

Nobody talks to my father. He sits beside me in silence. He listens. From the corner of my eye I can see that he follows my words. He reacts to them mostly smiling. The Patriarch is listening! What's going on? A part of me that never grew up, the small boy that appears from time to time, especially in front of my father, is amazed. That boy inside me—the one who waited his whole life for his father to listen to his words—can't believe this is happening. But now, that same little boy is not the same grown-up who doesn't need a father to take care of him anymore. I talk and he hears a summary of all the years of my schooling, traveling, experiencing things . . . I tell stories I brought back home from the world I got to know, and my dad listens to every word. The nurse listens to me too. The doctor is doing her best. She's not a listener. She's a talker. But what is perplexing and most important to me at this moment is that my father tuned in. He takes in each and every word I utter. Wow! This is the first time in my life that he's quietly listening to me. But right now, at this moment, it's not what I want. I don't want him to get to know me under these circumstances. This is neither the place nor the time for the beginning of our communication. There's not enough time left for our story to start. This is not the time for a beginning! What if I start to like it—even the possibility of communicating with him? And what if it turns out to work? Will I then miss him more once he dies? What if both of us suddenly start to miss each other? This isn't right, says the pessimist in me. The optimist answers: come on, better late than never. If I give it a chance maybe the father I yearned after my whole life, the father I missed so much, and dreamed about, imagined him my whole life, would come into being just for a moment. The father who listens to his son's words, sentences, entire stories: the father who talks to and with his son. The father who asks, *where are you? Do you have enough to eat so far away from home? Are you afraid? Do you love me, Son?* Maybe there's time. Maybe there's time to get to know each other using his illness as a vehicle. Maybe the illness will soften him. Maybe it will change him. The illness that many managed to fight and some who even won the battle, but only a few who really managed to survive. Although not living the same life they had before the uninvited illness came along. But just like my father, having no choice, they all had to find a way to accept it.

34.

We're driving toward the doctor's office. It's in Trsat; in that eastern part that, when the river that divides the city was the border, was Croatia—in Sušak. Near the place where my dad had the house, which he sold because he had to help the family members who were in need. *I wouldn't have this one in my house,* says my dad thinking of the doctor with the curly hair, *she talks too much.* I'm driving and following the road. Wait a minute: the fact that someone talks too much is a drawback? A person who delivers monologues is flawed according to somebody who talked his whole life and shut up only after the doctor, his daughter-in-law's friend, told him that they were going to cut out a meter of his bowels? When the shit literally hit the fan. Go figure.

35.

You don't need to walk me inside the house, he says when I park the car outside his gate. *But I want to*, I say. *No, I don't want to be a burden to you*, he replies. He gets out of the car. I look at him, and watch how he walks, how he disappears around the corner of the house, to his basement apartment where, together with my brother's mother, after he banished himself from a luxurious house in Trsat, he first decided to hide, and then to die.

Back in 1986, I recall four years after I enrolled at the university, he called my stepfather—my mother's husband who, together with her, helped me throughout my studies, and asked him when I would finally graduate. And I was still on schedule. Bogo, that's my stepfather's name, told him something like: *unlike you Vasko, I believe in Niko one hundred percent and I'm not in any doubt that he will graduate in time.* And using the opportunity that my dad handed him on plate, he intelligently humiliated him once again. See, here in the Balkans, when a man takes your woman away from you, regardless of whether he does it just to screw her or to marry her, it's a disaster. Not only does wife snatching strip you of your macho pride, but it also makes your dick shrink by at least two centimeters. And I'm talking here about an irreversible process. So, after my stepfather humiliated my father by taking my mother away from him, he humiliated him once again by expressing his trust in me, convincingly adopting me, at least for the moment, , and thus taking his son away from him once again.

That's not how I meant it, said Dad when I communicated the fact that I was writing my thesis day and night and that I was about to graduate and that, in fact, I had a job waiting for me in the National Institute of Lexicography. I asked him why the fuck he didn't have any trust in me and why in the world he allowed my stepfather to humiliate him. *No, they made it all up. I was just afraid that you'd end up a lazy, unemployed bum.*

36.

Aside from being a relic of his communist upbringing, unlike the classical myths, my father's myth of the working-class hero being the ultimate hero with almost supernatural powers, has no foundation in reality. How can it have any foundation to begin with? It can't for the simple reason that it doesn't contain a remote resemblance to a myth. All my life I kept trying to understand that grand narrative of The Patriarch—the Worker's Story. Here is what I've figured out so far: the worker is a self-sustained, fulfilled, independent, and accordingly, self-sufficient category. The worker belongs to a class of individuals who can take care of themselves entirely. He should know, can know, and does know how to take care of himself. He doesn't need anybody's help. A lazy one, a nonworker, or "a drone" as Dad used to call them, is the one that needs help. For him, being a drone, life is very hard. A drone is broke. He earns no money. Because he earns no money he has no money. Because he has no money somebody needs to give him some money. And from my father's viewpoint, this is not an easy life. The worker, on the other hand, has money. He has money because he works. Therefore, it's logical that the nonworker has every right to ask the worker for support. The worker has and thus must give money away. Especially to a family member who happens to be a drone. The drone has no money and, unless helped, can't be of any use. A worker works. A nonworker doesn't work. Dad loves workers. Dad doesn't love nonworkers. A worker. A nonworker. He loves me. He loves me not. Dad loves workers. Because they're not in need. Dad doesn't love nonworkers. But he understands that they're in need. A worker. A nonworker. He loves me. He loves me not. Dad loves workers. Dad doesn't love nonworkers. A worker. A nonworker. Dad loves me. Dad loves me not.

You'll rip the flower to shreds playing that "he loves me, he loves me not" game, my son warns me. *I love him,* continues my son, *I love that drone of yours. If you were a drone, you'd be at home with me all the time.*

37.

Saturday evening, we returned from Bakar. Tin tells us his stomach hurts. Jasna and I don't know what's going on. Is the pain he feels real, or does his little body respond to all the illnesses that surround him? We look at each other with a question mark hanging loosely over our heads. Have we been talking about illnesses too much lately? My uncle has cancer. It's lung cancer in its fourth and final stage. Both his lungs and his pleura are almost gone. My father has colon cancer. It has spread to his liver and to his lungs. Simo, a close friend and fine writer, is dying of kidney cancer in Zagreb. Tin and I visited him. The two of them played basketball in Simo's hallway. Simo was better and won. We should stop talking about sickness in front of the child. He's only four.

Tin asks me where in fact do I work. Is it the university where I teach or is it the newspaper where I write poetry reviews? I tell him I work in both places. Columns I write at home, and my lectures I prepare in my office. *I see,* says Tin, *and what do you teach?* Ever since he was a small child, not even two years of age, we talked to him the way we talk to grown-ups, so I decided to continue in this way. *I teach ethnic, national, and racial identities. I-d-e-n-t-i-t-i-e-s* he spells it perfectly, *what are "identities?"* I tell him that identities are made of qualities that make me who I am and make him who he is. *I see,* his eyes reflected in the rearview mirror of our car are wide open, *how many identities do you have,* he asks. *One,* I answer. In fact, I went for a lie just to make things simpler. *Just one,* Tin is suddenly disappointed, *but that guy in The Incredibles has five identities. Five, how come,* I ask. *Yes, five, exactly five,* he answers. *And what are those?* I ask. *I don't remember,* he tells me. *You should see the movie.*

38.

Today, for the first time in two years, Jasna went to see my father all by herself. I've actually given up on counting the years. Our separation, my father's and mine, has affected her immensely. It has hurt her much more than she's been willing to admit. Our separation, my father's and mine is affecting her immensely. It hurts her much more than she's willing to admit. In most cases, tenses are of no help. Future tenses predict, past tenses reminisce, and this one, the present . . . this is all that happens in-between. It's somewhat like an in-the-meantime tense. Left without a choice, we call it and feel it, we act in it and react to it as: the present. The one and only present we have. So, let's make the best of it! Let's all go see Dad!

Going there is never easy after years of separation. The last decision to vanish from his life was entirely mine. I believe that it's easier to endure a separation if you're the one who makes the decision to leave. It's especially true in the male world—in the world of fathers and sons. In situations like mine, like ours, the father is usually at fault. I might, of course, be wrong about that. There's always the possibility, the probability one could say, that one is wrong, and it makes no sense to deny it. Why did we part? What caused it? What was the trigger? Hard to tell after all these years. I recall only the tools and means that made our separation possible: words, selfishness . . . and a prick. Yes, his cock was the particular tool that was the reason for our separation. First he decided we ought to measure our dicks and compare sizes. And once he got the first set of results, which could easily be calculated in centimeters, he thought that the only right thing to do was to continue the dick comparing game for the rest of his life. If lived in a less patriarchal world, we'd be pissing together. Not like in a game: pissing in each other's direction. *Testa a testa.* No! Together. *Insieme.* The way it's usually done in the Balkans. The younger one pisses in the toilet bowl while the older one urinates in the basin. Then, over the course of the years, while pissing, we could see whose is bigger. After that, one would flush his piss down the toilet while the other would wash his urine down the basin. Like all grown-up men should do.

Tired of the pissing contest I decided to move away, not too far, but far enough to be invisible. I moved away and returned, vanished and came back regularly—until now. And now I decided to disappear forever. I know that to make a decision is one thing and to be able to endure its consequences is entirely another thing. Pain is incommensurable anyway. Unless it's the pain seen through my brother's eyes. Or his mother's for that matter—it makes no difference at all. That thought of incommensurability stayed with me this first night in Trieste.

39.

How is he, I asked Jasna when she came to Trieste with Tin. I was through with my lectures. Claudio went back home, or to Turin, I'm not exactly sure. The three of us were walking through a strong, subalpine northern wind better known as bora. I thought of Nevera, the Italian partisan from Claudio's novel, *Blindly*. If the wind was this strong in World War II, how the hell did anyone manage to win the war in this area? The partisans must have been heavier than the Nazis, because, man, it wasn't easy. I'm a two hundred pounder and this sucker lifts me up in the air every third step I make. And the partisans . . . we were told in schools, they had all kinds of enemies. The Nazis, collaborators, internal enemies, external enemies, the Ustashi, the Chetniks . . . they had to build an entirely new system, Socialism, they had to bring industry and electricity to the entire country, they had to restore education, build a new world . . . and on top of all that . . . bora. Dad always claimed that the army was the only place where all people were equal. He had in mind the Yugoslav Federal Army system—the one in which we, all the teenagers, had to serve. *If they're all equal,* I asked, *how come some command over others? There must be an order, and there's no order without a hierarchy. Especially in the army,* he said. *A hierarchy among equals,* I wondered. *How else, you idiot? What was it that you studied, philosophy . . . whatever it was that you studied . . . it was in vain. You didn't get jack shit out of it.*

40.

My dad was always allowed to do whatever he wanted until very recently. It was because he was mostly drunk, and no normal person wanted to mess with him when he was intoxicated. Now he's allowed to do whatever pleases him because he's sick. Because no one in their right mind sees any sense in contradicting a terminally ill person. I wonder how much freedom he's going to have once we're all certain that he's about to die. Then he will literally be able to do anything. Things he never did before. Like dying.

41.
Ten years have gone by since I was last in Trieste. I'm back. I stay in a hotel named Posta. Back in the '80s, it was the place where all the underpaid Croatian writers slept when holding readings and book signings. Today, the hotel is completely remodeled. I doubt that the Croatian writers would be able to afford this hyper-modern place nowadays. It's gay friendly too. Croatian writers aren't gay friendly.

I learned about Posta from a friend of mine, a famous Croatian writer who was once almost shortlisted for the Nobel Prize, at least that's how the story goes. They dropped his candidacy after the rumor had spread that he himself wrote his own letter of recommendation. This is just one among many stories going around on a rather dysfunctional national literary scene. In the '80s, I was here for a conference and I needed a place to stay for the night. I was a part-time journalist then, reporting from a writers' meeting discussing the interconnectedness between the process of writing and translating. The big names at the event were Umberto Eco and Claudio Magris. It was right before the war, and the radio station I worked for was rather poor, so they couldn't afford to give me an allowance. I had to find the cheapest possible hole-in-the-wall just not to walk the streets all night. Today the writer, Nelko is his name, is in Rijeka. He became very famous in the meantime. And me . . . I'm here, in Trieste. Today, he's an icon, sitting at the conference whose sole topic is himself. He just turned seventy and almost every city in Croatia decided to pick a date to celebrate his birthday. Today is Rijeka's turn. With all the cities lined up to party it feels like Nelko has a never-ending birthday. Upon my arrival in Trieste, hearing me talking about him to my host, the translator, Tin asked, *how many birthdays does Nelko have?* His question resembled a situation that had to do with the day the Pope died. I remember, Tin wasn't even two, and CNN kept repeating the news about the passing of Pope John Paul II. With his eyes glued to the TV screen, Tin kept repeating, *the Pope died again.*

And now, *no per forza dunque, nella terra di nessuno,* I am forced to go to a no-man's-land, as one of Nelko's characters said in his famous novel, *Exercising Life*, an Italian trapped in Tito's Yugoslavia in the post-World War II period, waiting for a train to take her back to the country of her origin—to Italy. I am thinking of Nelko and Claudio—the two eyewitnesses of the border experience. The way it looks to me, standing in this abandoned tram stop in Via Carducci, the two of them just intersected, each being an abandoned wagon on the circular railroad of our intertwined histories. And myself? What about me? Being both here and there, I know less and less how to depart and where to arrive. Can I depart at all? Can I use the border to divide myself in any productive way? Can this division I'm not running away from be a way to make me one whole and fulfilled individual?

My father too is on the way to crossing the border. And I am here. And I imagine myself to be that character from Nelko's novel, that Emilia girl. I see myself being made of paper and letters for this occasion, just like she was for the occasion of the collective exile of the Italians from their Fiume. On which side of the *frontiera* am I right now? Maybe it's a good idea to remain Emilia for the occasion. Paper made.

42.

I was in Posta ten years ago for the second time, in some sort of self-exile. I left my country. I wanted to act quicker than those who were thinking of kicking me out, or of just putting me in a uniform and sending me out to die. I said to myself: no one is going to kick me out! I'm leaving. So I kicked myself out. The funny thing was that, a few years later, in Chicago, I met a young scholar who organized a panel discussion. The topic was the phenomenon and dynamics of self-exile. He asked me to take part. No, I told him, there's no point having me talk about it. I did it. But he was persistent. He said that precisely because I did it I was the perfect candidate to add some juice to the entire scholarly discourse. I hate it when Americans treat me as a specimen, as the object of a case study, as a roaming informant, in fact, as a guinea pig. In refusing to participate, I explained that my talk, even if I were prepared to divorce it from my own experience, would necessarily include criticism of my country. And that's something I refuse to do outside my country. I criticize Croatia only in Croatia. And I do it for the love of my country. Unfortunately, that kind of love and care—the one expressed through criticism, cursing the injustice, bitching at the criminals in power— is utterly incapable of being grasped by the majority made up of flag wavers and anthem-screamers. But I'm not tired of exercising that kind of love. Not yet, at least.

43.

The last time I stayed in Posta, I was on my way to the States. Today I'm on my way to the University of Trieste. Then I was writing about the book Danube. Today I'm giving a lecture together with the book's author. Claudio and I, *testa a testa*. And all of it, like every dream that once becomes reality, feels so unreal.

Why am I writing it down in this way? Why am I bragging instead of waiting for someone else's recognition? Why am I putting myself in harm's way, being so self-absorbed and egotistic? Am I after all my father's son? I know this is not a nice way to do it. I know that it's even impolite. But I also know that I would never have done it if my dad, the way fathers, I imagine, should and must do, had told me just once something like, you're good, you're not ugly, you're smart, you're honest . . . you know what kind of phrases I'm hinting at.

Such words, those I never heard my dad say, are meaningful. They don't refer to small and insignificant things. They are the fabric of life that, if you hear them as a small child, is spread out before you. But, if you don't hear them in your childhood, or if you don't hear them at all, then you're forced to make your own patchwork of self-recognition and sew it on top of the fabric your self is made of. They're all hollow, self- aggrandizing, annoying to listeners . . . but what's most important is that, in spite of the fact that you yourself chose the time to utter them, they always come to you too late. Sad and in a stupor, left alone and abandoned, just like Frankenstein who, all alone, his boots planted on the polar ice, gazes straight into the nothingness— the same void all our fathers emerged from to take possession of us—and screams out loud, louder than the snow that's covering his long black coat, *father, you made me but you didn't tell me what to do!* The same as Pinocchio's story, but this time with uglier characters made of many more parts than Geppetto's wooden doll.

Exiled and sheltered in the uncertainty of the world, in the '90s I decided to gather up all the knowledge available, all the languages I could assemble, all the idioms I needed so desperately in order to write an analysis of Claudio's book. Today, the two of us—two colleagues—speak together. And neither of us assesses or judges anything that is ours. And, note, he is someone's father too.

Exiled and sheltered, self-exiled, I managed to survive in the world. Today I know exactly why. For the sole reason that nobody gave a flying fuck about me. The world didn't give a shit. That's precisely why it's called the world. Unlike the homeland, which always wakes up feading on its citizens' deaths thus proving its profound and serious concern for them, the world as a whole is completely indifferent. While providing room for anonymity, it gives one the sense of security and freedom. While I was altogether elsewhere, back home, first they counted the blood cells, then, they sorted them out using the nationalist criteria that can't even think of dividing blood from the soil, and finally they decided to drain all the blood out—not only from the owners—out of the entire country—in the name of the country. A country so self-sufficient, in love with its misery, enamored of its xenophobic singularity, its uniqueness that can't survive a simple comparison. While inside the country, the outside disappeared; outside of it, that very country is nowhere to be found. Although I do recall a party in San Antonio when a priest from former Yugoslavia, was he a Serb or a Montenegrin, for the life of me I can't tell, asked me *what is your blood*. I looked at him, raised a tall glass filled with Bloody Mary, and answered in a flat tone, *B+*.

My life in exile was simple. Simplified. I had only one wish—a wish that, being unfulfilled for a small eternity, became an obsession. This obsession of mine was so strong that I almost fell in love with it. All I wanted was peace. First I wanted for the war back home to stop. I envisioned something like a truce, and then I wanted a greater peace. I wanted death to get tired of us and to leave us alone. We alone have no capacity to scare it away. I was convinced it was up to death to tire itself out.

Those who come back . . . us who return home, we insist that there is a continuity. Actually, we stubbornly hold on to the illusion that there is such thing as continuity. And we build it upon the unremembered. On something we, in order to survive, first invented, then beautified in the eyes of memory. And then, when that part of our job was completed, we decided to hide it away from ourselves. We put it in a safe and secure place so we could find it once we returned. The way we imagined it to be, it was something very much private, and ours alone—our handy, portable reality—a reality so beautiful that, in the absence of our own present, could make the present of our homeland.

44.

Dad once came to Venice to see me. I was there in a hotel with two sisters, actually twins. One of them was a scholar in Italian studies and the other was some kind of a Wall Street broker. They were both from New York. Twins though, they were hyphenated—Italian-Americans. The broker loved to watch her sister fuck me. Once she joined us. They left just a few hours before my dad showed up at the hotel. The moment he entered he asked me why I got such a big room and with so many beds. I told him about the twins. *Go fuck yourself,* he said, *why did you send them away, Son. We could've fucked them together.*

45.

The homeland, once you've left it, appears in non-verbal ways, echoing the sound of a rapid heartbeat that the locals can't really hear. It shows itself in a set of useless repetition of words that the locals interpret as your clumsiness within the language you have found yourself surrounded by. It manifests itself in compulsive and repetitive moves your body does while they interpret you as one in need of their help. It unmasks itself in the clichés you use out of necessity—the clichés that annoy every single person you meet; even those who are your closest friends. It also annoys the police, tellers, IRS clerks, the notary public . . . it reveals itself in biting your nails in public, in pushing your closest friends away, using sentences like, *what, you want to fuck while back home people are dying?* . . . It all takes place, I feel, because history, an individual history at least, hides itself inside memory. In its pit it feels safe, protected, covered . . . and hidden in such a way, it finds ways to inscribe the fact on your body—the fact that highlights yet another fact—there is no logical, natural, happy, and quiet end. The end hardly ever follows the deeds that precede it. It's not part of the process; it's self-sufficient and always real. Reality, we have witnessed it more that once, requires no logic.

Regardless of the difficulty of remembering things, I am going to work today. I know I can do it. Although, I shouldn't allow myself to be to relaxed in front of Claudio. I remember once, in a suburb of Ljubljana, just after I defended my PhD, my father telling me—a glass of wine in his hand—*Son, remember, any determined fool can complete all the school requirements. You're either born a man, or not. Here*, he raised his glass, *I congratulate you on your doctorate!*

Today, the two of us are colleagues. Not my dad and me. Claudio the teacher and me the pupil; Claudio my topic and me his executor. And I remember now, it was twenty years ago in the bar at the Esplanade Hotel in Zagreb, Claudio was writing a dedication on the first page of the Croatian translation of *Danube*. In the dedication he called me his co-traveler down the river. I am indeed his co-traveler. But not down the Danubian region this time. Now it's the mutual journey of two travelers.

Claudio and I agree on many things in the course of our talks. Actually, sometimes it feels as if we are in complete accord with one another. The eyes of the students in the lecture hall remind me of my own former eyes—of the way I used to open them wide, listening to Claudio twenty years ago. Before the war, when I was far from being Claudio's co-traveler, and felt like a child in front of him. And that child I am talking about, survived.

See, there's always payback time for those who manage to survive! For the stubborn.

46.
All I need are the two of you. Today Dad and I walked through
Rijeka. Once we reached the National Theater building, my
brother took over. Then the two of them walked. I don't know
where they went or how long they strolled. I ran home to cook
dinner. I was making bacalao.

While cooking, my father called: *I need emotional support.*
Nothing else. After today's walk, I'm strong enough to endure
everything. OK, we can walk every day. We can walk twice a day.
We can walk all the time but our walks won't stop the world
from spinning. Neither will the illness inside him stop growing
and devouring him. They will race in pairs, two by two, while
we walk: the illness and Dad, Dad and the world, Dad and his
liver, Dad and his lungs, Dad and his brain . . . all that worldly
matter until the world wins and continues to go on, leaving my
father down and under. But that's not fair. It's not fair to talk
about eventualities and the passing of time when your balls are
caught in a vice between now and eternity. But there's not much
we can do about it, is there? In our culture we never talk about
death. As if death is not an essential part of our life. Our exit.
The only final and definite thing we can count on. A return,
perhaps, who knows? A disappearance. A continuation of life
in a different mode? The departure? The end? Nothing at all? A
whisper? A whimper? A howl? A bang? Silence? An exhalation?
All our lives, while we remain silent about it, each and every
one of us imagines death in his own way—a way whose content
matches the mode of death's silence.

47.

Dad decided to cremate his body. His decision has nothing to do with him being an atheist. Or does it? Who knows? Because, during communism he was an atheist, and, I recall he strictly forbade me to attend Bible studies, or to go to church. Bible studies took place on Sunday mornings, and I remember how lonely I felt while all my friends were in church. They came back home with candies. In the churchyard they played table tennis. My father didn't allow me to join them. Even though my mother's side of the family was somewhat religious, their members being mixed, Roman Catholic and Serbian Orthodox, he didn't even allow my grandmother to baptize me. I later had trouble because I wasn't in possession of a piece of paper that tells you you're baptized. A sacrament, right? See, I fell in love with a Catholic woman who wanted to get married in church, and almost every priest I asked to marry us fucked us off. So I had no choice but to find a crooked one. Thank God, it's not too difficult to find a corrupt scum in the sacred community. And it was an old former communist party official from Rijeka who, after the nationalists took over, and after Croatia signed a contract with the Vatican, practically making our country its non-secular dominion, the Vatican's miserable colony, decided to become the official church publisher, it was he who found me a priest who was as crooked as they come. The priest was eloquent, extremely intelligent, and extremely nationalistic. His xenophobia, homophobia, and nationalism were closely related to his blood alcohol level. After a bottle of brandy he was a part-time Ustashi. But it was he who made it possible, and Jasna and I got married in a church. She out of belief, and me out of my love for her and respect for the other. My old man was tough on the church. He showed no mercy until the '90s when, out of the blue, he started observing Christmas, Easter, and all that other stuff that made up the content of his former hate. My father's Christmas comes a little later, in January, if I'm not mistaken. At the beginning of Croatian independence, back in the '90s, he celebrated his Christmas in silence. He himself wasn't sure whether the president, Franjo Tudjman's nationalists were more out to get the atheists or the Serbian Orthodox.

But that's not the reason for his cremation. Him becoming ashes is purely for economic reasons. And for reasons of space. Together with his wife, he purchased a burial plot. And since they lived above their means their whole life, trying to show off in the community, just like everything else, the plot they bought was inadequate. It was a tiny plot in the cheapest of the city's cemeteries, which could only fit two caskets. But its lack of space could be compensated for. If some of the dead were prepared to give up their horizontal position in a casket, the plot could fit up to six urns filled with ashes. My father had his plan: when the time came, we would all fit inside the plot. Once again, he would step aside and put himself in an urn. So those in need of space could stretch out. His wife for instance. All her life she was fond of lying on sofas. She decided she shouldn't change her habits. A casket suited her. And my father was obsessed with stuffing all of us inside our burial plot. Therefore, he opted for an urn. We weren't able to get together while we were alive, but we'll be together once we all kick the bucket, he used to repeat while drinking some cheap brandy in the cellar of his luxurious home—the home he sold without saying a single word to me about it. He, of course, didn't ask my brother or me whether or not we wanted to be in that burial plot. He decided it without asking a single question—the same way he made all the decisions. He never asked us whether or not we wanted all those apartments and houses they kept buying and selling, always using the same excuse: We're doing it so we can have a place to gather. And we're doing it so we can have something to leave behind after we depart. He repeated this mantra until he sold that big, luxurious house in the suburbs and moved to a small apartment. And, as you know all too well by now, he did it because there were some in our family who needed assistance. The jobless in need.

48.

Dad got the CT results. The cancer has spread to his lungs. Officially it says that the findings suspect there might be secundarisms. Does it mean that the cancer itself is a primarism while the metastases are secundarisms? So what will the cause of my Dad's death be in the end, a primary or a secondary one? And how precise is all this to begin with? If the cancer is a primary and the metastases are secondaries, then the one that settled in his lungs should be called a tertiary, because the first metastases already devoured his liver. And who knows what awaits him next? Usually it spreads from the bones to the brain, and then can we talk of quadriarisam, of quintianisms. . . what's going on here? Or perhaps the linearity of its progress is not the right way to try to understand the invincibility of cancer?

49.

I'm better, says my father. The ultrasound shows evidence of improvement. *I only have two scars left on my liver, each less than two centimeters in length.* I know about his lungs, Dad doesn't. I'm not telling him. I feel like shit because of not telling him. Actually, I don't know whether to tell him or not. I know I should tell him. But I also know that he won't get jack shit by my telling him anything, except for fear and sorrow, both made of the same fabric his illness is made of. They're almost palpable. You can feel yourself losing control over your own body and how it's slipping away from you. It's so out of control that the very word control withdraws from your active vocabulary, and moves inside the pit of nostalgia. And it happens when this flesh we're all dressed in starts abandoning you, when, day by day it becomes less and less an integral part of you. Left without a choice, you convince yourself that all that's happening is happening in your head. Everything but the body. It resides outside your head. And this head-body divide is exactly what Christianity is based upon; not only Christianity, philosophy, and fishing as well but it's hard to say exactly why fishing fits in. It's there, outside of you, where the story about you is being told . . . never properly named, never completed.

50.

I'm shitting and bleeding, just like my father. But it's because I had too much red wine and therefore I have hemorrhoids. So, after all, it's not similar to my father's case—this blood that's dripping out of my ass won't kill me. While shitting, I stare at my swollen feet. I'm too heavy for my size and age, I say to myself. The stuff coming out of my ass is horrific. I was expecting to see some shit but not this kind of stuff. It's all bloody, creamy, juicy . . . you could almost serve it as a mix of red and black caviar in some cannibals' café. I was trying to put together the thoughts about my own shit. I was observing the human-made horror when my son, a sleepy head, entered the toilet. *Dad, the brandy you had sucks ass. You stink!*

Tin's lecture immediately reminded me of an episode from a long time ago. I think this was the first time that my father frightened me. We were coming back from a swimming competition. Our brother, the third one, the one who hung himself, won the race. He was the fastest, swimming fifty meters freestyle. I was happy, delirious. I was happy because everything else that guy did, sucked. Sheer terror lived in his skin. It was a mixture of his own fear of being in the world and of the fear he (probably in defense from the world) spread all around him. On our way home I noticed that my father wasn't walking straight. He was tipsy. I wanted to check the level of his sobriety, and asked him: *Dad, which sport is the most difficult one? Jerking off,* he answered. The brandy he'd had that day sucked ass. He stunk.

I was so frightened at that moment that I promised myself I would never drink in front of my own kid. I was nine. Today, Tin reminded me of my promise.

51.

I'm still on the can. I'm tearing the toilet paper into pieces. *Ame—debrame*. He loves me—he loves me not. Like that flower game that helps you try out your luck with someone you fall in love with. He loves me—he loves me not. A worker—a nonworker. I tear it into small pieces. He loves me—he loves me not. To tell him or—not to tell him . . . about the lungs, of course.

52.

Language is a cock-sucking son of a bitch, an asshole . . . plain crap, a coward that hides behind its own imagined objectivity. And the way it gains that objectivity is via precision. On its way to precision it doesn't follow the route of poetry, no, it goes for the route of lies. This is how language does it: the innocent kids killed in a marketplace in Kandahar are referred to as collateral damage. The body found with a bullet hole in his head is referred to as the target. The criminals and the crooks that, in the name of our country, robbed our country are referred to as controversial entrepreneurs. When a mass killing takes place language jumps in calling it Operation Iraqi Freedom. The slaughterhouse that marked the end of the twentieth and the beginning of the twenty-first century is called The New World Order. The Mafia killings done by bullets and bombs are called messages.

The thing that will kill my dad, that same fucking language calls secundarisms.

53.

Will I miss my father once he dies? I don't know. In fact, I never had the time to get to know him. Those who see things through their own eyes will say that it was my fault. Others who see things through my eyes will say that it was his fault. So, having their own way of seeing things, neither party will ever know the real reason why my father and I never got a chance to get to know each other.

When I try and think of all the things he taught me how to do, I can recall only one: he taught me how to tie my shoes. And he did it in a very peculiar way. Some would say that the way he taught me how to tie shoes is entirely wrong. I saw other people tying their shoes "the proper way," but I was persistent. I continued to do it my dad's way. And I did it on purpose. I had a clear reason for it: whenever I did it "the wrong way," I felt I was with my father. He taught me how to tie them. And to tie shoes "the proper way" . . . any determined idiot can do that.

54.
He has a checkup in two days. They did the MSCT. The cancer has spread. Dad's lungs are riddled with metastases. He has a hard time remembering things and keeping them in order. He can't remember the exact date of his checkup. In reality, the date and time of his checkup changed just once. But this isn't the same reality he lives in anymore. Or perhaps they changed his checkup date twice? I don't remember either. Perhaps I'm making up my own private reality to survive this mess.

55.

How long will it last, he will ask himself once his doctors confront him with the fact of his imminent death. Will they just blurt it out, or will they hide behind the linguistic apparatus of their profession? Will they use the neutrality of language to mask the information, making it less personal? He could live up to five years, I was told. But everything I know is based on statistics and has nothing to do with my father. And what are statistics to begin with? A line of numbers whose percentage is there to assure or destroy hope? In this particular instance, a hope that my dad can live a little longer—a few more days or months . . . but what kind of a life is he going to have—what quality of life is ahead of him? A life one would want to live? Or a life that one, once here, has an obligation to endure, because life is the way it is, one and unique, or simply because God or Nature commands us to live it despite the sufferings. Because, you can't enter your own grave alive, as my friend's dad once said just before he died. He too died of the same kind of a cancer my father has—colon cancer. He was in such fuckin' pain that even his newborn granddaughter was getting on his nerves just because she was lying next to him. The funny thing is that he kept prolonging his life just to see his grandchild being born.

56.
How long will it all last?

I don't know, I practice the answer just in case someone asks me.

How did it all start—this illness of his that we became aware of three years ago—after he started bleeding—after he wiped the blood from his asshole using toilet paper, not telling us a single thing about it? Was it his illness? Was it our illness? Who knows? Be it his illness or the one we both share, in both cases it's incurable. By now, his illness has its official name: colon cancer that, bypassing the lymph nodes (since every cancer is smart enough to find the shortcut of its choice), spread first destroying his liver and then shut down his lungs. Our illness—the one we have in common—is a chronic and constant misunderstanding. It's based on the fact that we don't know each other. Its symptom, the way it manifests itself in my dad's case, is the male Balkan homegrown insecurity that, in its mimicry, masks itself in aggression . . . instead of going into seclusion it rages, putting down everyone who approaches in a set of surreal confabulations that make an endless line of lies, of rudeness . . . That illness can also be an excuse for drinking yourself into oblivion. It can be the reason why, in denial, the ill one decides to build parallel worlds. It can even lead to some kind of a paranoid schizophrenia. This last sentence almost makes no sense. It, in fact, is just a social anamnesis I use to sophisticate the simplest fucking selfishness, and I have no idea why I'm even looking for an excuse for it. But I know that selfishness itself, his selfishness, was the reason my father was simply useless.

57.

I returned to my father after two years of being incommunicado. It wasn't the first time I'd left him. Although I used to leave on an off just to protect myself, to survive and to look for ways to be good to myself and to others, this last departure was a unique and memorable one. What makes it unique is the fact that, upon my departure, I was a father too and I knew exactly why I left. I left because he told me I was a bad father. I left because I had to protect both myself, and my own child. The way he saw Tin was as if he were his own toy—the toy that I just participated in creating, almost like a mediator. I came back after I read an SMS from my brother while I was on a business trip in Beijing. Afterward I had to go to Shanghai and then I flew back home. I waited for a few days to gather the courage to enter the hospital room. He was lying in his bed, looking at me and at my brother. He was lying still. Without even turning his head, he looked sideways . . . I saw a tear in his eye, and he seemed to say, *you don't need me anymore. You're both grown up now.* And it was then that I wanted to kill him! I wanted to kill him without a drop of blood on my hands. I wanted to kill him using my head, my thoughts, my imagination . . . all the weapons I kept building and maintaining all my life . . . I wanted to kill him with the only thing I really knew how to use: my imagination—the same imagination that helped me throughout all these years I spent convincing myself I really had a father.

58.
I returned to that sad and unfulfilled relationship. I have no idea whether there's any love left in it. What I do know is that the love, together with my father, moved out of my life back in 1969 when he drove away in his white Fiat 750. It was the second time he'd left us. I didn't see him leave the first time. I found out he was gone when I saw only two plates on the dinner table. *Where's Dad,* I asked my mother. *He's gone,* she said not even looking at me. *Then I'll wait for him to come back,* I said. *The food's getting cold, eat,* my mother said. *So what if it's getting cold? I'm not about to eat without my father,* I said. *Then you won't eat for a long time,* she said, *Niko, your dad's gone. No, I won't eat,* I said almost choked by sadness.

I didn't eat until I turned eighteen.

Today, when Jasna looks at the snapshots from my childhood, she opens her beautiful eyes wide saying, *what the fuck man, you were an anorexic* . . . What the fuck did I know what that word "anorexic" meant at the time . . . everyone just called me Skeleton.

59.

I returned to that relationship, hoping that the illness would make my father a better person, that it would draw his attention to the essential reasons why we, being here and now, are the way we are. I was hoping the illness would teach him the value of life—even of that barren one, the core surviving part of it that is the basis of any possible fulfilled life. But it didn't happen. His gossip, his fabrications, his plain lies, and his malice . . . his total disregard for anyone but himself, his selfishness . . . his emotionally crippled ego . . . were maintained with the same zeal. The cancer bypassed all of these. It knew only too well how to stay away from the enemy it couldn't defeat.

60.

Three days before the checkup he called my mother out of the blue. He asked her why I was turning my son against him. And my son is only five. Needless to say, even if I wanted to, I simply have no clue how to turn a grandson against his grandfather. And when I was a small child, my dad used to say terrible things about my mother. Perhaps he thinks I learned something from him. My mom left him. And to be left was never on his agenda. He couldn't cope with it. *Your mother, Niko*, he used to say, *is a drone, a whore* . . . and I was only nine or ten. It was back then when he took away those two books he gave me for my two tenth birthdays, so I'm not too sure how old I was when he told me that my mom fucked other men. And he told me that exactly after two years had gone by and I had no clue where he was. He simply vanished, and now, with the same ease, he returned. He decided suddenly to come back into my life just to tell me that my mother was a whore. So he must know only too well how to turn a child against his parent. But this has nothing to do with reality. I never said a bad word to Tin about his grandpa. I didn't even tell him that he fucked around on his wife, that in fact he's a drone and a fucking alcoholic.

The cancer was devouring Dad's body. His spirit remained intact.

I shouldn't have come back. He doesn't need me to take care of his body to begin with. The doctors do that. And the medication helps. And it was me who found and mobilized both: the doctors and the medication. After all, I might not be completely useless. He has ways to use me. He needs me to have someone to humiliate, to put down . . . to make me feel useless while mobilizing his words against me. And that was precisely what he did for most of his life. Now we've both simply gotten used to it, and it's too late to change anything.

This is how he does it:

61.

—Why aren't you bringing my kid to me? (By "my kid" he means my son).

—I had no idea you were expecting him today.

—What was your idea exactly?

—You didn't tell me you were expecting us today, Dad.

—If you had any idea how much that child means to me, you would never have said a single word against me in front of him.

—Dad, you had two years to call him, and you didn't. You chose not to. You know that quite well; so don't start now with "how much he means to me" . . . and shit like that.

—I see,—his voice is becoming stronger, a real masculine, patriarch-like voice, natural so to say . . . he sounded like a real man if you know what I mean—you tell me— he continues inquisitively—perhaps you know the reason why I didn't call you for two years . . . didn't call you, not him!

—I don't know—my voice is weak, high-pitched, like a real pussy squeezed in a vice—maybe you just didn't care to call him.

—Listen, Son, our relationship will never be normal.

—You're right. It won't.—I confirm in a pussy-like voice— Dad, don't you remember telling me that I was a bad father . . . you told me that the day I told you how Tin was going wild all over the house . . . and later on, I figured out he had a fever and that was the reason he was so grumpy, going nuts . . .

—Fuck it now, man, it's your job to put him in his place, to bring some order in his upbringing.

—Are you fuckin' normal . . . the kid was only two.

—Well, your nephew was the same, and your brother knew how to bring him up in a proper way.

—I have no idea what he did to him, but that kid is great.

—See, why isn't yours great then?

—I don't know.

—Fuck all of your PhDs, and your philosophies, psychologies

. . . whatever the fuck you studied . . . is there anything you knew to begin with? Why did I put you through school . . . you fucking worthless moron.

—Do you care to hear what hurt me? Should I tell you just one of the many episodes when you put me down?

—Tell me.

—Do you remember driving me to the post office that summer I came back from the States?

—What fuckin' post office? Fuck you and all your post offices.

—I had to mail something to the university, remember, to Austin?

—Was it when you were still with that American girl who left you after you figured out a cabby was banging her brains out . . . the one who lived two doors away from you? Was it then, when you called me afterward to tell me that a taxi driver was fucking your girlfriend?

—Yes.

—So, what was the awful thing I said to you that time?

—Something like, if I did nothing besides spit in your face for the rest of my life, that still wouldn't pay me back for all the sufferings I endured, living seven years with your mother. And I endured it just for you. I didn't want to divorce her before you started elementary school.

—Fucking God . . . asshole, do you know how it was for me to be with her? I still stand behind every word I said to you. Grow up, idiot! Perhaps you'll understand how I feel . . .

—How do you feel?

—Like you give a fuck about how I feel. I, who was a secret police agent, and whose cellar is full of diplomas and awards, I who am a respected member of society . . . and my son has been running away from me ever since the divorce . . . and everyone knows me . . . I'm somebody, Son . . . and people laugh at me . . . do you get it? Are you normal?

—I have no clue. I think I actually am normal. Dad, I was

only seven years old when you and Mom divorced. How could I have been guilty of anything?

—Fuck you and all of your university degrees when, after being in school your whole life, you don't know whether you're normal or not. "I think I actually am," what kind of an answer is that?—My father started mimicking me in a childish baby voice—Did anything else hurt you so terribly . . . tell me so I won't die without knowing it.

—Yes. When we came back from the United States, among other things, to be closer to all of you. Nobody was getting younger and I decided that perhaps it was time to come back. And you had an extra apartment in the house and didn't offer it to us. You had an entire floor of your house that you could have emptied, but you had some tenants there, and I came back with a pregnant wife with practically no place to stay.

—Fuck me man, like you would have agreed to live with us.

—I guess we'll never know since you never offered. And we were expecting a baby.

—See, the same old shit's happening again. You don't know. You don't know and you decide to fuck with me by telling me what I haven't done for you. But, tell me, because this is the way I read things between us, did you actually get angry with me that day when I said that Croatia, the way it looks now, would never enter the European Union? Remember, I said it to your father-in-law and he got kind of upset. Fuck man, don't you know we were drinking that day? We were smashed, and I said what I said, maybe not thinking . . . but tell me, is he angry with me as well?

62.

I really am a good-for-nothing. He'll be dead any day now and I'll never tell him the truth about the two of us. The truth the way I see it, of course. I'll never look him straight in the eye and tell him everything. And this is so wrong. He shouldn't die without my truth. Not that I'm not trying, I am. When I'm at home alone, I practice. In case I were ever to tell him all I want to tell him . . . crushed by bad memories, gasping for air, turning in circles around the living room, I practice . . . This is how my rehearsal goes:

First and foremost, Dad, fuck you and fuck all that's yours:

How could you have left us back in '69 without a word? I didn't know whether you were alive or not for so many years. So, fuck you!

Why did you get so scared back in '85 when the commies came to get me, sending their police to my apartment? As a commie yourself, why didn't you protect me from them, your commies? Look at them! They're all around us! They're still alive and kicking, stronger than ever. They just cross-dressed and became nationalists. And they're so strong that they don't even need to invent an enemy.

Where are my savings you promised to give me after I turned 18?

Where is that famous letter that explains the reasons for your divorce? You promised to give it to me along with my savings. On the same day.

How could you sell the house without telling me? I was your son too. It probably happened because not a single part of that house was ever meant to belong to me. But, let me go back. See, I'm turning in circles, again and again, going back in time when you vanished from my life for the first time. When you left before you really and definitely disappeared. You left, remember, and I had no idea where you were until I saw an article in the newspaper saying you had a terrible car accident on the Santa Ana Bridge on the outskirts of the city. But that's not what I'm thinking of right now. I know that you left us being unhappy. I was unhappy too. I was so unhappy that I remember it all as though it took place yesterday. And I remember when and where I finally saw you for the first time. Before you were gone for good. Do you remember, Dad? It was you who came to the ceremony as the official party member to admit me into Tito's Pioneers—the organization every first grader had to join. The ceremony took place in the cinema hall in Bakar. We were all lined up on stage in front of the white screen that, they told us, for the occasion, represented the homeland altar. The same way today they line up the little altar boys in churches . . . it's the same old shit . . . Tito's pioneers, Christ's pioneers . . . neither of them knowing what the fuck they really represent because they're what they're told they are, regardless of their will . . . filled up with the emptiness of symbols chosen by their country so their lives can have meaning. Yes, you were there, representing the Communist Party of Yugoslavia. And without giving any sign of recognition, without speaking, you put a red bandana around my neck. Along with a blue cap and a small badge, the bandana was a part of the symbolic triad. Holy Tito's Trinity: one squeezing your neck, one covering your small head, and one pinned to the white shirt over your heart. I hadn't seen you in weeks. You hadn't been at home in weeks. We hadn't spoken to each other in weeks . . . and we used to be inseparable. We played together all the time. I remember once, my balloon exploded and I got sad. You took the rubbery parts that were lying on the hardwood floor of our bedroom in the Old Town, and, using those leftovers, you made two smaller balloons. They flew much faster than the big one over my head, erasing my sadness. There you were on that stage. You were young and handsome and full of pride. As young and handsome and full of pride as you were on that day when, completely fucked up by pride and damaged by sorrow, you left us. There, on stage, you shook my hand. Yours was warm. Mine was sweaty . . . but I refused to let your hand go.

I didn't let it go. I wanted to hold it forever, there, in front of all the pioneers. You said, *Congratulations, comrade pioneer!* I had no idea whether there was something else you wanted to tell me . . . something aside from that automatic praise, *Congratulations* . . . the word, floating above reality, determined that surreal moment and sealed my own reality for the rest of my life. I too don't know what, if anything, I wanted to tell you that day, but I know that I was squeezing your hand until you, being all too familiar with the protocol, made a quick move, taking your hand away from mine. I don't know what I wanted to tell you, but I do know that I had something to tell you, that at least I wanted to. Instead, I started reciting the oath: *I promise to be a good and faithful comrade, I promise to respect my parents and all the elderly people . . . I promise to continue to march the sacred paths of the partisans . . .* Me, Tito's pioneer, with a red bandana around my neck—the bandana that, without a word, my father placed there. And what am I doing now? Did I keep the promise I gave that day? Do I really respect my parents and the elderly as I said in the ceremony? See, viewed altogether, it seems as though I'm the one who fucked it all up. It seems as if I'm the one who betrayed you, Dad. Me, who promised to be a good boy—me, the evil Pinocchio.

Let's continue. Why did you never buy me a single schoolbook? Fuck you for that too.

You never sent me a food package when I was in Zagreb studying.

Why did you humiliate us by sending the alimony month after month for over eleven years without once increasing it by a penny? Inflation was so high that, a few years into your alimony, it wasn't enough to buy me a loaf of bread and a bottle of milk. I lived with my grandparents, remember? My grandfather was the only breadwinner, and they had me to feed. My grandparents never sent back the alimony. Know why? Because, my grandma didn't want to humiliate you.

And why, once you finally agreed to share the cost of my

studies with my mother . . . why was your half of the allowance always late? It never came when it was due, so I had to humiliate myself and call you to remind you that I was still waiting for the money.

But, fuck all of the above . . . here's what really pissed me off: how in the world could you, without even knowing me . . . how could you tell me that I was a bad father?

63.

These words made me spin. I'm spinning in circles as they come back to me. Dislocated, fragmented, repetitive . . . they can't and won't make a whole picture because they're not whole. They're circular and they come back to me . . . returning to me against my will like some bad refrain from a popular song. The picture of horror never comes as a whole. Is this the way the horror in fact shields us from its force? It's hard to believe that though, because even though it doesn't come back as a whole, even though it comes to life only when multiplied, it keeps coming back over and over again. It keeps revisiting us until we puke, until we begin to peel it off our bodies, our muscles shaking, our skin sweating . . . our body convulsing . . . and when we convince ourselves that we could actually first freeze it and then expel it from us, then we choose words as our weapon to fight all the phantoms. But words prove to be useless. The picture of horror remains intact. It sometimes even strengthens, speeds up, and comes back when we least expect it, being stronger than ever. And then we're left with nothing but words. And these words repeat themselves. They multiply among themselves— they divide and start circling around us, making a circle that we seem to be trapped in and can't exit. Who knows why they call that inescapable whirl remembrance? Why do they call it testimony?

64.

See how much this child loves you? How much he loves his dad?
my father asks me, showing me a snapshot he took the other
day in front of the locker room of a local soccer team. Tin leans
against me in his too large yellow and blue soccer uniform. *One
day*, he continues, *you, your brother Robi, and I will sit and talk
about this photo.*

I'm reviewing the latest x-ray findings. There's no further doubt.

The metastatic wounds indicate dissemination of the disease,
and are in accordance with meta-changes.

65.

I literally bolted over to his place after he called, making it there in less than twenty minutes. He read the same x-ray results to me over the phone. *It means my cancer has spread. It's in my lungs now too*, he said with absolute certainty in his voice. Any hopes about the matter were now out of the question. *Yes*, I confirmed, *it looks like it has.*

While I was driving toward his apartment, I had to catch my breath. Poor man, I thought: helpless and left in ignorance about the level and seriousness of his disease, facing signs of finality that, once again, are couched in the language of someone speaking out of their professional domain.

What will I tell him when his wife opens the door? What will I tell him when I leave his place? My car is full of food. I was about to make chicken soup for Jasna who'd caught a cold. Should I tell him that? Should I tell him I need to go home and cook? Should I tell him about Tin, who just started taking English lessons at the kindergarten? Should I tell him about the fish I bought the other day and froze? Should I tell him to fuck all the findings and how we'll continue to fight the damned cancer?

Hey, my old man, I said when I saw him in the recliner, studying his findings. He was halfway lying down and endlessly staring at the white paper with so few words, *what's up . . . What's up*, he replied, *this is what it is, and this is how it is . . . I know what it is and what's in store for me.*

II

1.

I've organized everything. We'll go to Bosnia all together. Fine, I said to myself. We'll go! I haven't been there for ages. I remember a house in my father's village that had no toilet. It had one, but it wasn't an integral part of the house. It was a small wooden barn where you could piss and shit. Actually, the way I remember the house and everything that surrounded it . . . it was all wooden. My dad had two sisters. One lived in that village and the other one was in a city nearby. The city was Doboj. The village was Pridjel. And this Pridjel, that village, this is 'the village' my father has in mind whenever he calls the part of a city he lives in, 'the village.' He mimics the locals whenever he says its name. He does it by leaving the second vowel out. He swallows the 'e' sound so the name of his village sounds like it suffered from being a surplus value noun. And when the Bosnian locals ask, where were you while staying in Pridjel, you're supposed to say, I was in Pridlj. And then you're one of them.

All those villages, man . . . and that one in particular . . . so weird to a city boy . . . like that day when his peasant sister came out of nowhere, chasing her cows, her husband, a dog . . . who knows . . . maybe she just went to the field . . . I don't remember, but what I do know is that she locked us up in the house. She left while we were sleeping. Once in the village, you must take an afternoon nap, so I was told. We woke up and had to piss. We both had a tremendous urge to take a leak. I can't recall the exact level of that urge but I do remember that both of us were standing by the window screaming, *we protest because we need to piss.* I will never forget that camaraderie of our piss-filled dicks. My dad and I—two guys who didn't live together in the same house anymore, were standing alone, bladders bursting, in his sister's house, with no fuckin' toilet inside its walls. I remember that connection, that strong bond made of a yellow liquid that by no means was allowed to leak on the floor in their living room. I remember it and I will never forget it—all those funny shouts of ours and all the screams for help. *We protest because we need to piss,* was our mantra of the day. Up to now, we have never had the same quality encounter. *We protest because we need to piss,* we kept shouting, looking at a long line of apple trees in the orchard.

But it all took place on the first floor of the house. Why didn't we just open the window, jump out, and piss in that hole? No, instead, both of us decided to wait for my aunt to unlock us—our bladders swollen from the load of urine that kept increasing.

2.

Dad's wife left for the pharmacy. She went to buy some of those morphine patches. She passed through the gate like a ghost. She has some problems with her spine and that's why she's been in retirement ever since she was in her mid-thirties. Before her retirement she worked as an announcer in a mall. It was during socialism when the entire economy was based on so-called self-management. So, she too succeeded in managing herself by arranging for an early retirement.

I'm sitting by my dad's bed. He's asleep. Every now and then he moans. He lifts his left hand and points at the opposite corner of the room. *He's here, he's here, that motherfuckin', shitass cocksucker . . . he's here. Look at him. He's not about to leave my room. See how tiny the motherfucker is . . . is he eating at all my son, is he hungry . . . make him something to eat when he's here, let's not be rude to the shithead.* Dad gave up eating. And there's nobody in the corner of the room. My dad gave in and decided to replace his pain with hallucinations. We stick the patch against his skin every third day. Before, while he was in excruciating pain, he begged me not to put any patches on his body. He wasn't about to have any painkillers. *I want to be brave,* he said, *I want to die like a man.*

And after his diapers started to fill up with some disgusting brown liquid, urine . . . who knows what the body has to expel in order to protect itself from the side effects of chemotherapy, I remembered our rural camaraderie while being locked in his sister's house and had to piss so desperately. Our bladders were full of urine and there was no toilet inside the house. Now his bladder is full of some horrific stuff that signifies the nearness of death. His toilet is just behind the corner—that very same corner where that skinny asshole lives. But my dad can't go to the bathroom anymore. He looks at me with his small, bloodshot eyes and I can see that he's ashamed. He's lying on his left side, and I see a tear emerge from his left eye.

3.

When I, in fact, now look at the emptiness that has occupied the place of a conjunction, dad and I, I completely understand why, that day, in my aunt's house, neither one of us opened the window. And we were standing right next to it. On the first floor.

4.

When I, in fact, now look at the emptiness that has cocooned itself inside our mutual space—the space in between a father and a son—space that in all the solvable family crossword puzzles is simply called dad and I, or, some dad and some son . . . , or, either of the fathers and either of the sons . . . I'm not at all surprised that, while the brown liquid was oozing from his body and filling his diapers, and while his right shoulder was shaking out of control, I left the window of his first-floor bedroom closed. I didn't want to miss out on feeling that vibrant current of his impending death. I wanted to remember each and every part of it for the rest of my life.

I wasn't afraid of losing him at all. All he taught me was how to tie my shoes. And he taught me that in such a weird, almost sinister way. And I continued to tie my shoelaces his way all my life. I'm still tying them that way. I do it because I don't want to forget him. I do it so that, while I'm tying the laces together in one of the most insane and complicated ways in the world, I feel as if I'm close to my dad. And I've been doing it all alone. I tied them that way even in times when I had no clue where my father had moved to, leaving his big and luxurious home in the suburbs. I wasn't afraid of him. I'm not afraid of him dying either. I'm not afraid for one simple reason: he never taught me anything else. Even now, when his shoulder is shaking, and when his entire body is going crazy, shuddering from pain, he's not teaching me how to die. This very episode, his death, like the entirety of his life, is entirely his own. His, his, and only his. And this is how it's been throughout his life, while all the illnesses he knew belonged to other people's bodies, while they lived in the pages of medical encyclopedias, in conversations with his neighbors . . . with his guests in his villa he had in Opatija . . . I was never a part of anything that, he decided, belonged to him.

5.

My aunt is running after me. There's a chicken trying to run away from her. It's zigzagging. My aunt has a small axe in her hand, something like a tomahawk. The chicken is hopping. Actually, it trembles the way those down in Florida who are put to death tremble once they're hooked up to the nearby power plant, sitting on that electric chair. I watched an execution once. I was in Texas. They put a guy in the chair, and then they covered his head with a solid black hood, like those bags you get when you buy potatoes from an organic grocery store. Then they adjusted him in the chair a little better, and someone, wearing a uniform, turned some shit on, something resembling a knob on a stove, after which the hooded one started to shake. Smoke started coming out of his skull. And they showed this shit on TV, as if nothing serious was happening. And us, used to watching actors all the time, we were quite calm, tranquil. It's not happening to us, after all; it's happening to someone else. It's happening to someone who's neither you nor me . . . but the worst thing about it was the way they showed it. Without any context, emptied of everything: anger, remorse, empathy, revenge . . . It looked as if it wasn't happening to anyone at all—not even to the guy who was actually dying in front of our very eyes.

And that chicken now . . . it runs in circles. First in circles and then it chooses to run diagonally. Like it's some kind of a game my aunt and the chicken play all the time. For a moment, it looks as though it wants to hide in a shrub. Then it suddenly changes direction as though it wants to climb a tree. I got used to instant chicken soup and I couldn't care less for that free-roaming shit. Used to eating vacuum-packaged chicken breast, I couldn't care less for the chicken my aunt has finally grabbed. After cursing her entire family, including the unborn, she swiftly decapitates the chicken and now, all bloodied, is bringing its headless trunk home under her fat sweaty arm.

Niko, see, she's so completely fucked up. What do you want, the breast or the leg, my aunt celebrates the murder.

I stare at the chicken's head. Separated from its body, for some reason, it still trembles. Dad's body trembles. He puts his hand inside his diapers and tries to pull out his excrement. He's almost gone but it feels like the shame would survive him. I know that somebody has already written this. The one whose character ended up with a knife twisted clockwise in his heart. It all happened at the very end of the novel. I read it when I was sixteen. At that time whatever I read, I read the end first. Today I know almost every ending of every novel I've ever held in my hands. It's fair to say that I read more endings than the novels themselves. I remember that one with the guy with a knife in his heart. I hold my dad's hand. I look at him, opening my eyes wide, trying to signal to him that there's no reason to feel ashamed at all. Masculine toughness or feminine weakness, it's all one. There's dignity in all. Or there's no dignity. Who gives a fuck! In fact, fuck both masculinity and dignity. Fuck it when you're forced to dig out your own shit, shoveling your own ass with your own hands. And fuck that guy too. The one with the knife in his heart and the shame that, he thought, would survive him . . . fuck him. After all, he let them slaughter him like a chicken. Just like my aunt did the other day, killing the chicken whose head trembled, cursing its killer, or just laughing at her.

Dad's body trembles now, but it's not his entire body that trembles—various parts of my dad take turns in trembling. Now his arm goes crazy. His left arm. Just like the chicken's head. And now his arm is calm and his leg starts to shake. Then his right shoulder jumps. It all looks like a prelude to an insanely fucked up break dance.

I try not to look at him. I make an effort to think of simple things. Like, why when I'm with him can I never think of any actors?

Really. I know why. I started to hate actors in my youth, when his wife worked as a hairdresser in the National Theater. And my father loved to socialize with actors. He bought them drinks all the time, trying to buy their friendship. While they were good for his ego, because he felt good to be seen with famous actors in public, they were a disaster for his wallet. Behind his back, they laughed at him. All he wanted, I think, was just not to be alone . . . not to be alone once again, after the war, after the orphanage, after the divorce . . . no! And if a grab on his wallet was the price, who cares what it cost—two, three, or thirty brandies. I was running away from all of them. I was about twelve, I think, and already aware that my father was being humiliated and used. And it all took place while he was convinced the crowd admired him. *How can I love you when you don't allow me to respect you,* this sentence screamed inside me. I never uttered it. I never uttered anything. I was afraid of him. And everyone who knew him used to say, *your father is such a good man.*

6.

I was looking for words until I was sixteen or so. And then I started writing poetry. If you know how to do it—how to write poetry, I mean—then you don't really need to look for words. To write poetry when you're sixteen is not that surprising. Back in the '70s, almost all the sixteen-year-olds wrote some kind of poetry. I continued to do it in my forties. And that's what is so worrisome. Then, when I was sixteen, I went to Bosnia and my cousin told me, *man, if you want to fuck a girl around here you should never tell her you write poetry . . . if you write poetry around here they mistake you for a faggot, you know. So, don't be stupid. If you want to get some ass, you better skip that poetry thing. Tell her you play soccer or basketball . . . or, coming from the Adriatic, just tell her you're a sailor . . .* my cousin gave me this advice at a dance here in Bosnia. It wasn't a disco, more like a live band playing pop stuff. *Fuck me if there was a single poet in Bosnia who got laid bragging about writing poetry . . .* my cousin was persistent.

Dad and I went to Bosnia. He left earlier and I caught up with him a few days later. He stayed with his sister. I stayed at my cousin's place. He played soccer.

She told me she was nineteen as she lay down on some hay behind a wall, and after that, I wanted to say something that had to do with who I thought I really was at the time, just to give me the chance to get closer to her, to have her feel my breath. I told her I wrote poetry. *What, something like songs,* she asked. *Like songs?* I repeated her question. *Yeah, rhymes and that shit . . . Where do they sing it? Sing it?* I repeated . . . *Forget it,* she put her arms around my neck and whispered, *do you know how to kiss?*

7.

Dad's body is shaking. His left hand is removing something from his shoulder. That something he's after is invisible to me. I hope it's not that skinny asshole that hasn't left the corner of the room that's now sitting on my father's shoulder. Death filled the room. Did we have enough time, I asked myself remembering a scene from a movie. Unlike the guy in the movie, my father wasn't a Mafia henchman. The one I'm talking about was. And he was the Godfather. Time . . . maybe we thought there would always be some time left and we could use it when the right time came.

I remember, it was 1985 and my first book of poetry came out. Dad lived in Opatija. In Marshal Tito Street. It, of course, was the longest street in the city. *Bring those bums of yours . . . those who write the same shit as you so we can celebrate your book, all right?*

The official name of his house was *Vila Esperia*. Ten of us were sitting on the terrace.

I remember there was a water polo match on TV. We were playing Italy. At that time we were still Yugoslavia. It was about five years before the war. Being Yugoslavs, all of us sitting on the terrace that day, each felt in their own way as though we belonged to a big and colorful country. A country with all its languages that today have suddenly become mutually unintelligible despite the fact that, linguistically speaking, we perfectly understand each other. Except for Macedonian and Slovenian, which are distinct, almost overnight all the other languages that acquired their new names such as Bosnian, Croatian, Serbian, Montenegrin . . . are linguistically one single language. Politically, of course, they are four distinct languages. So, before we all became born-again polyglots, we all spoke one and the same language. We called it Croatian. Serbs called it Serbian. Yugoslav linguists officially named it Serbo-Croatian. Today, those same shitheads have become Croatian linguists. They vocally proclaim they never did such a thing. They say they never coined the term Serbo-Croatian.

We brought a TV out onto the terrace and, despite the fact that we were all Croats by birth, we cheered for Yugoslavia. Except for my father, who at the time was a Bosnian Serb and afterward, when it was a matter of survival for the non-Croats, he switched to being a Montenegrin. I have no clue why. But, whenever I think of him with affection, as someone caught in the misery of life, squeezed in between longing and belonging, I call him my father, and whenever I'm mad at him because he didn't protect me from my own misery and loneliness that entered my life after he left me, I call him Dad. It seems as if I mixed it all up. So perhaps he's right when he suggests that I'm a good-for-nothing.

Dad came out to the terrace. He was full of brandy, teetering on the edge of drunkenness. I saw him open his mouth, trying to say something. His tongue was plastered against his bottom teeth, and he looked like a monkey hanging on a tree branch searching for a banana. He was holding a black notebook. *Hey, you morons, he screamed, listen . . . listen to me motherfuckers . . . listen to what I wrote when I was an apprentice in Bosnia . . . I was studying to become a locksmith . . . a cocksuckin' locksmith, me . . .* We didn't respond. Our eyes were glued to the screen. The score was something like 8-8. *Fuck you assholes,* he continued to yell. Laughing out loud, he demanded we listen to what he wrote while at school. We scored. *You won't listen to me, you refuse to listen . . . but you read the bullshit my asshole son writes . . . don't you . . .* he continued to try to read at least one of his poems, which I had no idea he wrote. And perhaps being ashamed of his poems while sober, he decided to hide them inside his black leather agenda, a notebook that every man in socialism received at the beginning of the year just to be able to keep his schedule and all his obligations in order. They scored. And regardless of our disapproving silence, he started to read. His tongue lolled on his chin and he slurred the verses. The words rolled down the terrace like muddy water, saying something like . . . hips, water taking water inside itself, a teacher bathing in the river, naked, her pussy beautiful while she is pissing in the river. Bosnia was the river's name. It was a poem about a young and beautiful teacher he fucked, or wanted to fuck, while studying to become a locksmith. In the poem it says that he hid himself behind a tree, and watched her piss. She lifted her dress high and her cunt, described as something detached from her body, was pissing into the bigger body of water. Was it the Bosnia River or some other river that inhabits one of Dad's many planets that are unknown to me. I'm not sure.

We scored and won. 10-9.

In fact, I don't claim to remember the exact score, but I do think it was 10:9.

Dad's having problems breathing. His wife is in the kitchen. She's quiet most of the time. I know she doesn't know what to cook anymore. Dad's not eating at all. A few days ago, something thick, and the strangest color I've ever seen, dissolved by chemicals and the chemo drug Xeloda, burned a hole in his pajamas.

Fuck such a life, Dad whispers. His accent has come back, all the way from his childhood. He spoke in a thick Bosnian accent, as if he weren't lying in his bed in Rijeka but speaking from the house whose picture was hanging above his bed—the same house we were locked in once, unable to take a piss. *Are you in pain*, I ask. *Of course I am, it hurts like hell, Son, see, I'm dripping wet . . . What the fuck is leaking out of me . . . I'm lubricated . . . Niko, you hang out with all those writers, and among them, my father is gasping for air while his eyes roll around like a giant wheel in an amusement park, there must be some faggots among them . . . bring one so he can buttfuck me wet and slippery. I'm . . . ready . . . lubricated . . .* I know he's trying to make me laugh.

But the fact is that I don't know one gay among our decent writers. I doubt he would believe it. And, the fact that there's no single gay person known to me among the Croatian writers makes our scene suck. Actually, it might perhaps be a genuine tragedy of our national literature.

8.

What the fuck, man, who taught you to tie your shoelaces this way, she asked, watching me put my shoes back on, sitting on the hay after I'd just had the first great sex of my life . . . at least that was how it felt back then. So great, so amazing . . . It was all there: the hay, her, three years older than me . . . and being more experienced, I was convinced it was completely natural to lie back and let her do all the stuff needed for a good fuck to work out. She was kissing me, licking my ear, pressing my lips, and pushing her meaty and cold tongue down my throat . . . at one point I almost vomited while trying to fight back . . . I had my two front teeth broken in a fistfight, so whenever I returned her tongue lashing moves I kept producing weird whistling sounds . . . at first she looked at me as if I was completely insane, and after a while she got used to it . . . her hand was jerking my cock faster and faster . . . I remember her legs, her kneecap, her milky white ass, and plenty of sticky liquids in places I didn't expect them to be . . . And I . . . I was . . . what was I doing to her? I have no idea because, after I left, she told my cousin, my aunt's son who was her age . . . *fuck that lame pussy poet of yours, he didn't know how to put it in, so I had to do it all by myself . . . I had to shove his dick inside my cunt . . . Is he still here?*

It's so beautiful when your father is dying. Then you can suddenly tell stories like this one to everyone without even thinking about what effect they'll have on listeners. What could possibly be heavier and more real than your father's death? What is a story, regardless of its content in comparison with your father's death? In Bosnia, from where, a few years before I was born, my father, being a Boy Scout, came to Bakar . . . whenever they want to say, "can," they actually say, "you're allowed to." So, not only could I have said anything I wanted, but, according to their word choice, I was also allowed to do so. Now, when I'm allowed to say whatever I want, I return to memories and activate those among them I didn't dare to share before.

Here is a benign one: my father claimed he was a Bosnian all his life until one summer in the late '80s—one of the last peaceful and quiet summers before the war tore Yugoslavia apart, smashing it into pieces. He went on a trip. He must've had a feeling that his country would vanish soon and he had the need to see it in its entirety for the last time. While coming down the Lovćen Mountain where there is a mausoleum with a big sculpture of the great Montenegrin ruler, intellectual, and writer, Petar Petrović Njegoš, my father identified with his greatness and glory that dwell in that holy place, and decided to become a Montenegrin himself. Suddenly it sounded more appealing to him than his former Bosnian identity. He did it because he could. He was allowed to choose. And aside from living in a world of his own creation his whole life, there was some beauty in the identity swap he made that day. Ethnic affiliation, that identification usually mistaken for identity, is involuntary by default. It comes with the territory. It has to do with your heritage, place of birth, language, roots . . . and has nothing to do with your free will. And that's exactly what my father swapped that day: he became a Montenegrin because he identified with the greatest icon of its culture: Petar Petrović Njegoš, the ruler, the writer, the intellectual.

And I wanted to tell you this one too. If I were to embrace my Bosnianness that includes some Montenegrin elements incorporated in my sense of self by my father's choice, then the story about my fucking in the hay should go like this: Oh, how beautiful it is when your father dies. Then you're allowed to say out loud even words like hers, *fuck that lame pussy poet of yours, he didn't know how to put it in so I had to do it all by myself . . . I had to shove his dick inside my cunt* . . . And you can even do it in public without thinking about the consequences.

In the end, I didn't go to Bosnia with my family as my father planned. I fucked up again. And that Njegoš guy. He wasn't all that great. His epic poem *A Mountain Wreath* describes the heroism of the Orthodox Montenegrin tribe protecting the bulwark of Christianity against the bestial Ottoman Turks. This is the official version. In reality it's a manual for genocide, filled with bloody descriptions of violence that promote hate while trying to market it as self-defense. And rumor has it he died of syphilis. I think he overdosed on identity.

Forget Njegoš. I didn't go to Bosnia because of the power of illness. Illness is neutral. It has no favorites. In its usual slow approach, it indiscriminately decides to attach itself to each and every one of us. Sometimes I'm not sure whether illness is just like death: is it one, definite, and unique phenomenon that moves from body to a body, or does each and every one of us have his own unique private illness? One such illness, whose nature was then unknown to me, decided to leave my father's place, and after walking up and down the hills of our city, it crossed that bridge that used to divide Croatia from Italy—the uncivilized ones from those civilized, and sneaked into our apartment in the western part of Rijeka. It entered our home saying it wasn't the first time it had been among us. But this time it's serious. So I couldn't go to Bosnia. I had to stay at home. The illness embraced my wife's body and it has lived with us ever since. It would never go away, the illness promised. And living together, the three of us, Jasna, Tin and I, eat with it, watch movies with it, we travel with it . . . we sometimes even play together, the four of us, taking it for granted as the fourth member of our family. But that time, the time my father went to Bosnia for the last time, we couldn't travel. Jasna was in hospital and I was alone with our child. Dad, he asked me one night before falling asleep, how did Pinocchio manage to grow up without his mother? We were lying together in his single bed, and, after I heard his question, I had to get up, hide in the bathroom, and cry. It was later, almost two years later, when Jasna told me that on that night she had a near-death experience. I told her about the Pinocchio question. She told me about traveling in reverse through a tunnel with a bright white light at its end. And it was so beautiful, she said, I wasn't afraid at all . . . quite the contrary, it was almost pure joy.

I was there, I saw my family, friends, I saw them all . . . I saw my village and now I can depart, my father said. *It's a pity you weren't with us,* he said, showing understanding for my reasons for staying with my family. It appears as though my father and I filled in an application for a freshly devised happiness-sharing-program-within-the-limits-of-time. Both of us seem to be less clumsy when dealing with sorrow. There are even moments when we're good at it. Before I had to leave, I sat on the floor wanting to tie his shoes. He immediately lowered his body and sat next to me. He placed his foot on the step, gently moving my hand away from his, *Fuck man, what do you think, I don't know how to tie my own shoes?*

9.

I'm sitting in my aunt's apartment in Doboj. My aunt is crying. I'm sitting in my aunt's house in Pridjel. My aunt is crying. My cousin, the one who in fact arranged that by now ancient hay-fuck, is pouring plum brandy into a small glass.

Plums all around us.

Some of the houses that used to be here before the war aren't here anymore. Some of the people who used to cross the road in the village before the war don't cross the road anymore. The road has turned into a bridge . . . just like the bridge back home in Rijeka— the bridge my dad's doctor talks about when she talks of the great divide.

How's your wife, my aunt asks, *how's your child? Are they healthy?*

I nod to confirm everything is in order. I look at my watch.

And this is all that's left of Bosnia for me.

10.

Today I came to his place late. He's surprisingly quiet. It all seems to be in perfect order. He's not shaking. It looks like he's not in pain either. He's even freshly shaved. He shaved his head too, so the white hairs that were turning my father into someone else's relic are gone. But the most important thing is that he really doesn't seem like he's in pain. I approach him, and, once certain that the pain isn't there, after a long time I gather the courage to take his arms and lift him a little. I actually manage to put him in a sitting position. Then I take a piece of cloth and dry his forehead. I move his hand aside gently. I'm afraid it could get stiff from the heaviness of his body leaning against it. He's quiet. He even closes his eyes after long time. For some reason, he never wanted to close his eyes. They would circle the room, probably trying to locate that skinny guy who, my father was convinced, became his roommate. And, now he's given up gazing at that cocksucker who moved into his room. It's been an eternity, or even longer, that the two of them have shared the room. I count the hours that skinny ass has spent with my dad and I suddenly get furious. I feel a mixture of hate, sadness, envy . . . I'm not so certain what I feel right now. How should I feel wondering, was he real or not? That asshole spent more time with my father in one month than I managed to do in my entire life. Unlike my dad and me, he and his newly acquired roommate had their continuity.

Well, can I blame the skinny ass for that? I'm not sure. Nobody kicked me out of my father's home. I deliberately chose to leave, but you already know that. I could have come to visit him. I was both allowed to come, and not allowed at the same time. What if it was all my fault, I'm thinking while drying my father's forehead. It's pointless now, but I must say it again, nobody really kicked me out! After I realized that I couldn't make myself go there, that I simply couldn't start walking in the direction of his house . . . it was then that I kicked myself out.

Dad's sitting up in his bed. His legs are stretched out straight and, after many months, he's able to keep his spine upright and erect. I imagine him sitting the same way while writing that beautiful poem about the teacher he was in love with, spying on her while she was dipping her beautiful feet into the river. My proud father, a World War II orphan, who lost his father in the first days of the war, was in a kind of state-sponsored boarding school, studying something that had never been his choice. The state then was in need of blacksmiths and he was unlucky enough to be chosen to fill a spot. He was on his way to becoming something he never wanted but was allowed to become—a blacksmith. I imagine him sitting up straight and writing poetry. His eyes closed, his mind in search of the images needed to build the verses that would end up in a poem. In my imagination, trying the impossible— to reconstruct a scene I've never seen, his eyes were closed the same way they're closed now. And if they were open right now, he would have seen me, while looking for that long-lost image, in fact searching for my father.

He smiles at me. I take his hand and put it slowly inside his winter jacket. It's September and it has cooled down. I am so happy that my father isn't in pain that I decide to hug him. While giving him a hug, wanting to get as close to him as I can, I lose my balance and I jerk his body. His head leans forward and loudly slaps against my forehead.

Oops, says my brother, who was slowly putting his hand inside father's winter jacket, *does it hurt? It surely doesn't hurt him*, I say. We both smile for a second, using laughter as a means of pulling away from our father's head—the head he couldn't move anymore without us helping him. *Don't bend his hand*, my brother says, *it's getting stiff . . . let's not break it. We're almost done*, he continues, *the only thing left are his socks. His ankles are way too swollen. We can't tie his shoes.*

11.

I had a handsome father. It's very important to have beautiful parents. It's especially important when you're a child. I see his beauty even now when all his pain is behind him and when he's moved to some other place unknown to us. His face is calm. It has suddenly lost all its wrinkles and puffiness, and has become smooth and young, younger than ever. Much younger than it was on the day I returned from China. Now, after he has gone, there is one less thing standing between me and eternity.

12.

I saw my father's face for the last time when they came to take his body to the crematorium, efficiently placing it into a gray plastic container that looked like those plastic boxes commonly referred to as thula that upper-middle class people put on the roof racks of their cars. And the thing they boxed my father in was also a sign of something—a symbol of his own choice to burn. Just like a thula is a statement, my dad's box is a statement. He'll travel all the way to Zagreb in that box. To be cremated is a statement. It's a clear message to all those awaiting resurrection. In order to come back, they need to preserve their bodies. Without his body, my dad will end up in an ashtray. And it's there he'll remain from now on. He'll be left on a side shelf in the family plot. So that the others, who will hold on to their bodies, can fit in caskets. After all, it wasn't my father who decided to go for a burial plot. Faced with the decision others made for him, he gave up. He gave up the same way he is now giving in, while making room for the others.

Here she goes again—my flying grandmother. *Why are you swaying back and forth like a chimpanzee,* she criticizes me while showing she cares. *You're swaying like a monkey; there must be something wrong with you . . . Niko, see, he sways all the time like he's on drugs . . .* my grandpa Niko looks at me through the reading glasses both of them shared, and continues to read the newspaper headlines. It says here they found that ship that sank in the bay in the times of D'Annunzio . . . he tells my grandmother while turning another page. *Can't you see the question mark at the end of the title . . . did you give up even on reading the titles until the end,* yells my grandma while he looks at me and wrinkles his forehead. It was an old habit of his that he never had the patience to read newspaper articles through to the end. He only read the titles and, the older he got, he quit paying attention to exclamation points, question marks, periods . . . so he never really got to the level of interpreting titles for what they were. But he was so easy-going, so cool, so free of worries . . . calm . . . and I'm sure that his rejection of the myth of the importance of life, his stepping aside from accountability, which is so overrated, his making fun of responsibility, which many claim to have without actually proving it . . . all of that made him live a long and interesting life—a life so calm and filled with humor.

I'm standing in front of the urn filled with my father's ashes, slightly but rhythmically swaying, shifting my body weight from my left to my right foot. The line of people approaching us to express their condolences seems to be endless. I know that I must stand up straight, be still, and face the pain with dignity, like a 'real man', demonstrating the same strength and courage my father wanted to die with. But the line of people is moving past me too quickly, way too fast for me right now, and I can't pick the right moment to be still, straight, strong, and brave. They're speeding by me and I even smile to some out of confusion.

I'm outside of space and time right now, and I'm swaying and swaying . . . and there's my grandmother, flying above me . . . getting closer to me and bringing her face up so close that it gently touches my face. She picks me up gently, holding my shoulders, and makes me stand still. It feels as if she's planted me near my father's cherry-red urn that resembles a vase. She smiles and runs her soft fingers through my hair. She touches my cheek with her lips, and whispers in my ear: *Don't be afraid, he's just gone.*

13.

The line is endless. Listen, my brother says, *the trumpet player said he could play an extra song for the money we paid. He said he knows how to sing "Rijeka the Beloved" Shall we go for it? Of course,* I said, I hope he doesn't mess up the tune.

Of course we'll do it for our Dad. After all, Rijeka is his city.

III

1.

I'm standing in front of his grave. It's all behind me. There's nothing behind me. It's just very different now. This is, in some morbid way, so much easier—to come to him while he's ashes. If it were easy to visit him while he was at home, alive, I would have gone there more often. Like I am here today, at ease, without worries, without anything more to prove to him . . . calm. I can always come here. I can come whenever I want. Just like he always used to say after our arguments: You can come back whenever you want, you know that, Son . . . And I want to come here. And, as they would say in Bosnia, I'm allowed to. The only thing that's different now is that I don't have to come and visit. No one commands me to come to see my father. No more requirements, no more imperatives, no more assumed expectations. There's nothing I have to do anymore. For the rest of my life. At least nothing that has to do with him. The same way my son doesn't have to do anything that has to do with me. I decided once and for all that I would never pressure my child with any patriarchal shit. Because I love him I don't dare imagine that I have any right to posses him. And the confusion between love and possesiveness is one of the fundamental mixups in the Balkans. My son picked up all the collateral gain of the cultural dislocation and fruitlessness that is inherent to our uniquely flavored masculine infinitive must—a signifier without the signified.

There's nothing Niko must do anymore. Niko can do and

Niko does whatever he wants to do. And it starts today! Niko goes to his dad's grave whenever Niko desires, I can hear a child singing inside my adult body. When I go to him, the child inside me sings. When that child comes home, it unties its shoes, and after it returns to its grown-up body, they both sit and write it all down—both Niko and me. We do it like men, using our soft fingertips. The middle finger seems to be hitting the keyboard with a special zest. Like it doesn't belong to the rest of the fist. But most important things I type alone. I do it alone because Niko (the child that's telling you the majority of my story) shouldn't forget. Despite the fact that the verb must is finally behind him, he mustn't forget. And I do it for my own sake too. I type because I want to sense the pleasure of the sentence: There is nothing I have to do anymore! But there are so many things out there I want to do. Sometimes I want to write these two sentences using all the languages I know.

Now it's time to use that third bag and fill it up!

There were three of them, weren't there?

One bag full of blood.

One bag full of urine.

One bag full of nothing.

Once he'd died, I promised I would place him inside the third bag.

But he's been fried. He's been dismembered, crushed into particles, and scattered the same way my childhood in Bakar was; lost and scattered like my memories of him . . . nowhere to be found. The same way I was lost when my mom and her husband, after they married, literally snatched me out of my grandparents' hands and took me just across the hill to live with them in the city of Rijeka. They said they were doing it for my own good. They said Bakar was too small for me and I had no future there. But they didn't realize that I wouldn't have made it had my grandparents not given me all their love and embraced me after I was abandoned by both

Mom and Dad. Yes, my mother and my father left me behind, each in their own way. My mother came back with another man and I moved in with them, yes, but all my life my only real parents remained in Bakar: my grandma and my grandpa, a couple who reconfigured their lives in order to take me in and give me everything so I could survive.

2.

How come you never had the keys to your father's houses, apartments . . . Jasna wondered during our wedding preparations. No, indeed, I never had them, I smiled because, unlike her, I found the fact that I never had any of his keys natural and normal. That's just the way it was and I was simply used to it. I didn't know of any other way, and now, after thirty or so years, what is suddenly so strange about the fact that I could never open my dad's doors without ringing the bell?

Here I go dad. I'm going to place you inside the third bag— the empty one. I was keeping it just for you all the time throughout your illness. It's clean. But wait, it's not empty. It's full of nothingness. And that's not the same. To be empty is one thing, and to be filled with nothingness is quite another. If it's empty, it means that there's nothing inside it. Then you can fill it up all the way to the top, and seal it. Or it may stay half-empty. Or half-full, depending on who is doing the filling: an optimist or a pessimist. But if it's full of nothingness, there's nothing else you can put inside it. But I was saving it for you, not for anyone else . . . especially not for nothingness to take possession of it. But when you were lying in the hospital . . . with drip bags filled with blood and urine hanging by the side of your bed . . .
then I saw it the way it was—full of nothingness. And it was then when, probably affected by the image of you afflicted with cancer, awaiting surgery, that I confused nothingness with emptiness. Or perhaps I was so eager to find a place for you after you died that I confused the two—a bag that's empty with a bag that's full. And now, after I see the emptiness inside, how can I empty it? The bag is talking to us right now. It's filled with the same content that inhabited all the bags of our empty lives—with nothingness.

And I am sorry. I'm so terribly sorry. I am so sorry that the bag exists—the bag filled with nothing . . . because no matter how hard I try, I can't recall a single thing that happened between us. Nothing that I could point to and say: this made me sad and this is what makes me feel sorry today. There's nothing between us, Dad, except for the abyss full of things that could have happened, that should have happened, but that never took place. And this is where all my sorrow is—inside the nothingness. And the bag is full of it.

I frequent his grave, calm, with a smile, relaxed, and armed with newfound strength acquired through loss. I come here without the butterflies in my stomach I used to get whenever approaching his place. Those butterflies were ambiguous: they were in search of love, but also warning me that I might be hurt once I entered the house—hurt by Dad's words, threats, accusations, humiliations . . . all the tools he used in order to send me on a continual guilt trip . . .

The bag's full but it's far from bursting. I know that. Those hospital bags are solid. They're ship-shape, made in order to keep the ill from possible humiliation, while protecting the staff from the patients' diseases. But, hey . . . I almost forgot. There's still his ear left. And his bed that I promised to sneak into just before he died. I said I'd sneak underneath his sheet. And I would talk and talk until the last breath left him, telling him everything I ever wanted to tell him, everything I could ever have told him, everything I needed to tell him— everything. I planned on telling him everything I, as his son, was obliged to tell him, but, after I got tired of not being heard by him, after I lost the last hope that even repeating the same words, warnings, wonders . . . could have any effect on his ears, I remained silent. I wanted to talk until he finally kicked the bucket. Until he dropped dead, killed by my words, by my remarks that I wanted to shovel deep inside his dead ears . . . but I didn't.

3.

He's here. We're here. Somebody put his picture on top of the grave. In the photo, his head is swollen. It got that way gradually over years, adapting its shape to the amount of moonshine brandy he drank on a regular basis so he could escape life, up there, in the suburb of Trsat . . . in his cellar without windows, without air, without friends . . . His round head is looking at me. He looks straight into my eyes, and I'm not afraid of him anymore.

4.

I'm swaying from side to side in front of his grave, slowly . . . shifting my body weight from my left to my right foot. And he's there, fried, inside his cherry-red urn. I keep on swaying. There's nobody here to interrupt me, not even my flying grandmother. In fact, most of the time I'm completely unaware that I'm doing it. And I've been doing it my whole life. I sway as naturally and involuntarily as I breathe, as I piss, as I cough . . . I sway my body . . .

I didn't know the reason for that rocking of mine until one day, actually searching for articles on compulsive and obsessive behavior, I stumbled on an essay claiming that this kind of rocking from left to right . . . or the opposite direction, it makes no difference . . . is essentially linked to poetry making. I read that it has to do with writing poems!

It had to do with the same things my father, while learning the skills of a blacksmith, was doing as well. But he never did it in public. He wrote his poetry in hiding. He was afraid the tough guys he shared the place with might see him writing, and after they figured out that my dad was doing some faggot-like things, like writing poems . . . they would kick his ass.

Abandoned children have a habit of rocking their bodies. It is, in fact, a harmless thing to do, since the abandoned are capable of much worse things—like bullying other kids. Some of them, when they get older, even become killers, rapists . . . in-house tyrants. They beat their partners, sometimes even to death . . . the asshole language that allowed the secondaries to murder my father, softens the brutality of wife beating by calling it domestic violence. It locks it behind family doors, making someone's wounds their own private matter, and expecting it to resolve itself inside the house. Some of the abandoned children even fuck chickens, goats, donkeys . . . I knew of a guy who tied a donkey to the railroad tracks, turned a beer case upside down, hopped on it, and buttfucked the poor animal . . . he got so into it that he didn't notice the train coming from behind—and while he was banging the donkey, the train fucked them both up. Some of the abandoned decide to multiply. Shrinks call it multiple personality disorder. There's usually one among the many personalities who's in charge of the others, and who keeps all the personalities that inhabit the body of the abandoned one in order . . . He's usually referred to as "the keeper." I remember reading a book about a guy named Billy Milligan. He suffered a severe case of MPD and the funny thing was that his keeper was in fact a Serb. There were four of him living inside him . . . four dominant personalities and a bunch of smaller ones. They used to go wild, and I suspect that the fact his keeper was a Serb made him even crazier. Serbs claim they're a heavenly people, the smart and wise ones, who've inhabited the earth from the times that preceded the Big Bang. Perhaps this is what makes them good keepers. When Billy Milligan was a small child, he claims, his father used to dig a hole, throw him in leaving only his head above the ground, and piss in his mouth. He raped him too, on a regular basis.

You see how fucked up the abandoned can be. There's all kind of shit they're capable of doing. And they usually do it. So, all being said, this rocking of mine is nothing in comparison with what could have happened to me and I find it perfectly acceptable.

What's wrong with it? You're standing on your feet and you're rocking. You're not in anybody's way. You do no harm, and if you don't have a grandmother who gets all annoyed by your innocent rocking, you may live your life without even being noticed doing it. As unnoticed and invisible as you were on the day you first started to rock. As unnoticed and invisible as you were on the day you decided to produce your own private ritual music coming straight out of your small ailing heart. Frightened of life the way it changed and turned against you . . . but not frightened enough to disappear . . . you started to rock. And you did it hoping that your rocking would create the sliver of illusion of your presence in the world. Perhaps you also hoped someone would notice that change you decided to go for.

5.

I'm standing in front of his grave built perpendicularly against the ground, where the usual graves are supposed to be. In fact, it's a small concrete box. Its perpendicularity, in relation to the other, larger graves, somehow redefines and reshapes the dimensions of sorrow. I put my left hand in my pocket, searching for the car key. It's not there. I look in my right pocket, and it isn't there either. It's not in my jacket. I look around and it's not on the ground. It's gone, nowhere to be found. I stop rocking and the words start to rock instead of me. I'm looking for the key. I call out . . . the key, the key . . . where is my key . . . and I can't locate it . . . key, key . . . I keep chanting as if that would make it materialize. I release the words from my lungs. I spit them out of my mouth, and send them to look for the key . . . as if the cadence of the chant, once it leaves my lips and calms down my rocking body, moved into the space of the previously unspoken with a firm belief that from there, from that nothingness, it could solve the mystery of my lost key. What if I've lost it for good? How will I get back into my car? Where is my key? Key, key, where is my key . . .

As if keys had ears. As if my key could hear me. And even if it had ears, if it could have heard me . . . his loneliness, wherever it is now, by no means could match my own. The key doesn't speak. It produces no words Niko, Niko, Niko . . . And while I make my loneliness vocal, while I chant it, underscoring the loss of an object, I keep reminding myself of the insignificance of every single loss. Fuck the key. It'll be found . . . someday, somehow, somewhere . . . we can always go to a locksmith and make another one . . . two of them . . . a shitload of them. I may even have an extra key somewhere in the house, but that's not the point. While calling it aloud, I'm being blanketed with the materiality of words. The staccato of my chanting is not about to leave the repetitive and circular content of my search for the key. And that repetitive and circular search, along with my words and with my body, suddenly begins rocking. And in its rocking, it starts making circles around the flowers laid in front of my dad's grave, resembling a shaman-like ritual dance in slow motion—the intimate dance of two dead people. One of us being completely dead, while the other, just now, seems to be dead to a great extent. I only need to find that fuckin' key. And the moment I find it, I'll be able to tell you precisely who is who between the two of us.

6.

See, Dad, that's how poems come about. Not all of them. Mine did. Not all of my poems, but a great majority of them. Like those I've written but never read to you aloud. First and foremost because you never asked me to, and second, let's face it, Dad, what kind of poetry would it be and what would the entire literary history look like if sons were in the habit of reading their poems aloud to their fathers? You were aware of that problem, weren't you? And therefore you decided to protect me from becoming a lousy poet who reads his little poems to his dad. You, in fact, were indifferent just because you cared for the quality of my writing, weren't you Daddy? You did all you could just to protect me from others that might laugh at me after they discovered I wrote verses, right? You were protecting me by not caring for anything I wrote because you were afraid that if anyone found out that you followed my poetry I could have started rocking even more, right Dad?

The key, the key . . . where is that key . . . here goes a poem for you—the rocking one. It closely resembles, and I know it today, that self-sufficient rocking action, which hides inside itself the ultimate secret of disturbance. And who writes? We do! The disturbed. And you knew that. What a poem really is, is a translation of that subconscious lonely rocking—of that swaying back and forth that is emptied of any unnecessary movement just like any good literature is vacated of any unnecessary word. I will continue to write poetry and I will write a kind of poetry that will always desire to say something, but it will never be able to communicate the totality of that desire. And that gap between the desired and never uttered will yearn for my absolute presence in the world. It will scream out for recognition and respect. But it will be hermetic poetry, so no one will really get all this and nothing will change.

7.

Dad, hear how I mourn my misplaced keys. Hear how I curse my own mistake. Listen to how I celebrate it, announcing nothing but good news. All that is mine I based on the rhythm. First I gave myself to the rhythm of my body. Then I switched into the rhythm of my words. The key, the key . . . where is my key . . . I chant OK, but again, where did I put it? It's not here. It's not even close to here. But I have a replacement for it—the rhythm. The rhythm's taking care of me now.

From now on the rhythm is my keeper. It's not a word anymore.

With the rhythm on my side I can afford to forget the books I kept collecting throughout my life, imagining and understanding them to be the bricks I would use to build a fortress—the fortress that would shelter me from my own life. Yes, the rhythm took over and this is great. Now I can step out of my imagination and enter the world and rock back and forth like some feebleminded chimpanzee . . . and I don't care what others will say.

I start rocking and my key is gone. Forget looking for the keys. It's much easier to give in and devote yourself to the rhythm. The rhythm has a world of its own. And that world has its strict order. It spells out the rules that keep it together. The rules that make the rhythm-world alive are simple. They call themselves words and verses. And when I give myself to the rhythm, when I start rocking . . . I'm able to reveal all the reasons why I was angry with you my whole life. Actually, it wasn't you I was furious with, Dad. It was your words. I was angry at your words all along . . . until you died . . . and now things have changed. I am anger-free and I can come to you with ease . . . Sometimes coming to your grave even fills me with joy. Words, all the words, your words included, were the particles that made up the fabric of my life. They were the texture of my being—of its deepest and most profound rooms. They were everything: the keys, the key-owners, and the gatekeepers of my life. And now, liberated from those words, I can freely rock from side to side, like some sinister clown who, left with no choice, was forced to grow up overnight—the day you drove that small white car, first in reverse, and then straight down the steep slope, away from me . . . the key, the key, where is my key . . .

8.

I'm tired of being timid. Whenever I whisper almost soundless words—the near-to-mute sounds and tunes—things I expect to bring me back to life in its fullness, especially in its parts, I managetopollutethembybringingshameintothosewhispers. And I bring the most personal of all the synonyms of shame: lack of self-respect, a self-loathing of a kind. And I'm getting fed up with my rocking, with that feeling of being a numb, secondhand recliner made of flesh and blood and bones . . .

What do I get from all that swaying from side to side . . . what do I get from that rocking back and forth . . . I'm tired of aping only the allowed, the permissible, and the prescribed. I'm exhausted from mimicking things whose invisibility and remoteness makes them sound louder in the world we share. Like these motherfuckin' keys for instance . . . keys . . . they too sound so soft, their absence is a senseless murmur making the one who searches for them become as lost as they are . . . the key, the key, where is my key . . .

9.

Those rocking movements, those sounds . . . create the presence of others. Their presence feels very real when turning to you. But that presence talks to you in a very barren way. Its language is simplified and stripped of nuances. It's reduced to an elementary set of communication tools. That presence brings you back to your beginnings. It sometimes leaves you back there forever, motionless and affixed to just one and only place. But this is not all it does to you. There is also a surplus value to it. It creates a sense of strength—a strength you need so much to enable yourself to turn your head away from the most disgusting scenes of your past. It prepares you to refuse to continue remembering. And if it works its way to its end, it teaches you how to forget. Productive forgetting, a positive amnesia, letting things go . . . is a must if you want to befriend the past.

The invention of productive oblivion is important. It's more powerful and more useful than any bag filled with nothingness. Productive oblivion is full of tiny ritualistic images that, once written on your body, after being made of cadences, once inscribed in your voice, and then chanted out . . . can first displace you, then pick you up, and in the end, find a better place for you. And finally, once they're certain you're in a safe place in life, they have the power to transform your own memories. They remove all the pain from them and make them harmless, and you feel as if they've never haunted you. After their transformation, you feel as if the content of your memories was your choice all along.

Believe me, Dad, those particles of productive oblivion really want to help all those who are willing to accept the rhythm of their lives. And I choose to welcome them. And it will all work out. This time I know it.

In fact, to put it simpler, have you ever asked yourself why abandoned children only have selective memory? Why they choose to remember only the beautiful?

10.

And not to forget, there's a small lock called mimesis. It first enters your life as a lost symbol wearing a mask of a bare necessity, of something so essential to you that you can't imagine your life without it. For instance, the key, the key, where is my key . . . And that small private mimesis that you lock up inside yourself has its counterpart in poetry. And that's all there is to it. And it's good that things are this way. It's great that what took place between us took place exactly the way it did. I wouldn't have it any other way! It's great that my father never wanted to listen to my poetry. It's good that he never wanted to hear me out and make me happy just for a moment. I'm sure now that, had it all happened any other way, I would have never started rocking. And maybe I too, just like him, would have ended up becoming a blacksmith without making a single key or a lock.

Driven by sorrow, or by an extra sense of security that might have followed his recognition, I too would write my poetry in disguise, hiding my notebook under a classroom desk. Or on top of it, using my left hand to hide the content of my poems. In blacksmiths' jargon, poetry writing would become my part-time job—or a hobby. I would most probably write only when no one could see me. To see me writing might expose me to humiliation. There are always bullies around who think only faggots write poetry, and not only do they make fun of you . . . oftentimes they beat you up the way they do real faggots. The less aggressive, mature, and emotionally stable men know quite well that only those who rock their bodies write poetry. And those who sway don't even know where their keys are.

After I reconsider the life my father and I shared, I find my own life fulfilled, and under the circumstances, I see myself as a very happy man.

11.

I will rock now. I will start right now. And I'll speed up my rocking. I'll rock fast, so fast, the fastest I can. I don't care if I fall down and kiss the ground. If it happens, I'll get up and continue to rock. And I'll do it over and over . . . I'll repeat it to infinity . . . the same way I repeat words whenever I talk about the two of us—a son and his father.

12.

I'll repeat the movements until I repeat my entire self—after I rebuild it. Who knows how repetitive I could really be? I haven't tried it until now. And who knows what I'll learn when all this is over? Perhaps I'll find out that I'm as repetitive as my moves are. The rocking I mean, but you know all about it by now, don't you? Perhaps, while rocking, I repeat myself? So what if I repeat myself? If I learn how to repeat and rebuild myself, maybe I could find a way to repeat and reenact my father, and bring him back in a new, harmless, warm, and loving shape?

If it happens, and if I really reenact myself, I'll do it the same way I'm repeating my words while bringing them to life. Sometimes I even do it while speaking in tongues. I fragment the words, just like the memory of our domestic family horror is fragmented—the horror that is tamed, domesticated, and that first occurs as everyday, in-house dynamics, afterward turning into a matrix of a family where, almost overnight, from your father's son you become someone's father. It suddenly transforms into a family where you, not your dad, wear the pants.

Let it be that way. I will rock. And after a lifetime of practice, I'll become so good at it. You're free to call me an expert. And I'll rock with both of my feet firmly on solid ground. And no one will untie my shoes.

(Hald Hovedgaard, Denmark 11-20 June 2012)

Nikola Petković (b. 1962) is a writer, literary critic, translator, screenwriter, and scholar presently working in the Department of Cultural Studies and Department of Philosophy at the University of Rijeka, Croatia, where he also serves as the Chair of European Studies. In addition, Petković writes a weekly column on contemporary literature for the daily paper *Novi list* in Rijeka. He has published seventeen books, including works of fiction, poetry, essays, and scholarship. He writes in Croatian and English.

MICHAL AJVAZ, *The Golden Age.*
The Other City.

PIERRE ALBERT-BIROT, *Grabinoulor.*

YUZ ALESHKOVSKY, *Kangaroo.*

FELIPE ALFAU, *Chromos.*
Locos.

JOE AMATO, *Samuel Taylor's Last Night.*

IVAN ÂNGELO, *The Celebration.*
The Tower of Glass.

ANTÓNIO LOBO ANTUNES, *Knowledge of Hell.*
The Splendor of Portugal.

ALAIN ARIAS-MISSON, *Theatre of Incest.*

JOHN ASHBERY & JAMES SCHUYLER, *A Nest of Ninnies.*

ROBERT ASHLEY, *Perfect Lives.*

GABRIELA AVIGUR-ROTEM, *Heatwave and Crazy Birds.*

DJUNA BARNES, *Ladies Almanack.*
Ryder.

JOHN BARTH, *Letters.*
Sabbatical.

DONALD BARTHELME, *The King.*
Paradise.

SVETISLAV BASARA, *Chinese Letter.*

MIQUEL BAUÇÀ, *The Siege in the Room.*

RENÉ BELLETTO, *Dying.*

MAREK BIENCZYK, *Transparency.*

ANDREI BITOV, *Pushkin House.*

ANDREJ BLATNIK, *You Do Understand.*
Law of Desire.

LOUIS PAUL BOON, *Chapel Road.*
My Little War.
Summer in Termuren.

ROGER BOYLAN, *Killoyle.*

IGNÁCIO DE LOYOLA BRANDÃO, *Anonymous Celebrity.*
Zero.

BONNIE BREMSER, *Troia: Mexican Memoirs.*

CHRISTINE BROOKE-ROSE, *Amalgamemnon.*

BRIGID BROPHY, *In Transit.*
The Prancing Novelist.

GERALD L. BRUNS, *Modern Poetry and the Idea of Language.*

GABRIELLE BURTON, *Heartbreak Hotel.*

MICHEL BUTOR, *Degrees.*
Mobile.

G. CABRERA INFANTE, *Infante's Inferno.*
Three Trapped Tigers.

JULIETA CAMPOS, *The Fear of Losing Eurydice.*

ANNE CARSON, *Eros the Bittersweet.*

ORLY CASTEL-BLOOM, *Dolly City.*

LOUIS-FERDINAND CÉLINE, *North.*
Conversations with Professor Y.
London Bridge.

MARIE CHAIX, *The Laurels of Lake Constance.*

HUGO CHARTERIS, *The Tide Is Right.*

ERIC CHEVILLARD, *Demolishing Nisard.*
The Author and Me.

MARC CHOLODENKO, *Mordechai Schamz.*

JOSHUA COHEN, *Witz.*

EMILY HOLMES COLEMAN, *The Shutter of Snow.*

ERIC CHEVILLARD, *The Author and Me.*

ROBERT COOVER, *A Night at the Movies.*

STANLEY CRAWFORD, *Log of the S.S. The Mrs Unguentine.*
Some Instructions to My Wife.

RENÉ CREVEL, *Putting My Foot in It.*

RALPH CUSACK, *Cadenza.*

NICHOLAS DELBANCO, *Sherbrookes.*
The Count of Concord.

NIGEL DENNIS, *Cards of Identity.*

PETER DIMOCK, *A Short Rhetoric for Leaving the Family.*

ARIEL DORFMAN, *Konfidenz.*

COLEMAN DOWELL, *Island People.*
Too Much Flesh and Jabez.

ARKADII DRAGOMOSHCHENKO, *Dust.*

RIKKI DUCORNET, *Phosphor in Dreamland.*
The Complete Butcher's Tales.

RIKKI DUCORNET (cont.), *The Jade Cabinet*.
The Fountains of Neptune.

WILLIAM EASTLAKE, *The Bamboo Bed*.
Castle Keep.
Lyric of the Circle Heart.

JEAN ECHENOZ, *Chopin's Move*.

STANLEY ELKIN, *A Bad Man*.
Criers and Kibitzers, Kibitzers and Criers.
The Dick Gibson Show.
The Franchiser.
The Living End.
Mrs. Ted Bliss.

FRANÇOIS EMMANUEL, *Invitation to a Voyage*.

PAUL EMOND, *The Dance of a Sham*.

SALVADOR ESPRIU, *Ariadne in the Grotesque Labyrinth*.

LESLIE A. FIEDLER, *Love and Death in the American Novel*.

JUAN FILLOY, *Op Oloop*.

ANDY FITCH, *Pop Poetics*.

GUSTAVE FLAUBERT, *Bouvard and Pécuchet*.

KASS FLEISHER, *Talking out of School*.

JON FOSSE, *Aliss at the Fire*.
Melancholy.

FORD MADOX FORD, *The March of Literature*.

MAX FRISCH, *I'm Not Stiller*.
Man in the Holocene.

CARLOS FUENTES, *Christopher Unborn*.
Distant Relations.
Terra Nostra.
Where the Air Is Clear.

TAKEHIKO FUKUNAGA, *Flowers of Grass*.

WILLIAM GADDIS, JR., *The Recognitions*.

JANICE GALLOWAY, *Foreign Parts*.
The Trick Is to Keep Breathing.

WILLIAM H. GASS, *Life Sentences*.
The Tunnel.
The World Within the Word.
Willie Masters' Lonesome Wife.

GÉRARD GAVARRY, *Hoppla! 1 2 3*.

ETIENNE GILSON, *The Arts of the Beautiful*.
Forms and Substances in the Arts.

C. S. GISCOMBE, *Giscome Road*.
Here.

DOUGLAS GLOVER, *Bad News of the Heart*.

WITOLD GOMBROWICZ, *A Kind of Testament*.

PAULO EMÍLIO SALES GOMES, *P's Three Women*.

GEORGI GOSPODINOV, *Natural Novel*.

JUAN GOYTISOLO, *Count Julian*.
Juan the Landless.
Makbara.
Marks of Identity.

HENRY GREEN, *Blindness*.
Concluding.
Doting.
Nothing.

JACK GREEN, *Fire the Bastards!*

JIŘÍ GRUŠA, *The Questionnaire*.

MELA HARTWIG, *Am I a Redundant Human Being?*

JOHN HAWKES, *The Passion Artist*.
Whistlejacket.

ELIZABETH HEIGHWAY, ED., *Contemporary Georgian Fiction*.

AIDAN HIGGINS, *Balcony of Europe*.
Blind Man's Bluff.
Bornholm Night-Ferry.
Langrishe, Go Down.
Scenes from a Receding Past.

KEIZO HINO, *Isle of Dreams*.

KAZUSHI HOSAKA, *Plainsong*.

ALDOUS HUXLEY, *Antic Hay*.
Point Counter Point.
Those Barren Leaves.
Time Must Have a Stop.

NAOYUKI II, *The Shadow of a Blue Cat*.

DRAGO JANČAR, *The Tree with No Name*.

MIKHEIL JAVAKHISHVILI, *Kvachi*.

GERT JONKE, *The Distant Sound*.
Homage to Czerny.
The System of Vienna.

JACQUES JOUET, *Mountain R.*
Savage.
Upstaged.
MIEKO KANAI, *The Word Book.*
YORAM KANIUK, *Life on Sandpaper.*
ZURAB KARUMIDZE, *Dagny.*
JOHN KELLY, *From Out of the City.*
HUGH KENNER, *Flaubert, Joyce
and Beckett: The Stoic Comedians.*
Joyce's Voices.
DANILO KIŠ, *The Attic.*
The Lute and the Scars.
Psalm 44.
A Tomb for Boris Davidovich.
ANITA KONKKA, *A Fool's Paradise.*
GEORGE KONRÁD, *The City Builder.*
TADEUSZ KONWICKI, *A Minor
Apocalypse.*
The Polish Complex.
ANNA KORDZAIA-SAMADASHVILI,
Me, Margarita.
MENIS KOUMANDAREAS, *Koula.*
ELAINE KRAF, *The Princess of 72nd Street.*
JIM KRUSOE, *Iceland.*
AYSE KULIN, *Farewell: A Mansion in
Occupied Istanbul.*
EMILIO LASCANO TEGUI, *On Elegance
While Sleeping.*
ERIC LAURRENT, *Do Not Touch.*
VIOLETTE LEDUC, *La Bâtarde.*
EDOUARD LEVÉ, *Autoportrait.*
Newspaper.
Suicide.
Works.
MARIO LEVI, *Istanbul Was a Fairy Tale.*
DEBORAH LEVY, *Billy and Girl.*
JOSÉ LEZAMA LIMA, *Paradiso.*
ROSA LIKSOM, *Dark Paradise.*
OSMAN LINS, *Avalovara.*
The Queen of the Prisons of Greece.
FLORIAN LIPUŠ, *The Errors of Young Tjaž.*
GORDON LISH, *Peru.*
ALF MACLOCHLAINN, *Out of Focus.*
Past Habitual.

The Corpus in the Library.
RON LOEWINSOHN, *Magnetic Field(s).*
YURI LOTMAN, *Non-Memoirs.*
D. KEITH MANO, *Take Five.*
MINA LOY, *Stories and Essays of Mina Loy.*
MICHELINE AHARONIAN MARCOM,
A Brief History of Yes.
The Mirror in the Well.
BEN MARCUS, *The Age of Wire and String.*
WALLACE MARKFIELD, *Teitlebaum's
Window.*
DAVID MARKSON, *Reader's Block.*
Wittgenstein's Mistress.
CAROLE MASO, *AVA.*
HISAKI MATSUURA, *Triangle.*
LADISLAV MATEJKA & KRYSTYNA
POMORSKA, EDS., *Readings in Russian
Poetics: Formalist & Structuralist Views.*
HARRY MATHEWS, *Cigarettes.*
The Conversions.
The Human Country.
The Journalist.
My Life in CIA.
Singular Pleasures.
The Sinking of the Odradek.
Stadium.
Tlooth.
HISAKI MATSUURA, *Triangle.*
DONAL MCLAUGHLIN, *beheading the
virgin mary, and other stories.*
JOSEPH MCELROY, *Night Soul and
Other Stories.*
ABDELWAHAB MEDDEB, *Talismano.*
GERHARD MEIER, *Isle of the Dead.*
HERMAN MELVILLE, *The Confidence-
Man.*
AMANDA MICHALOPOULOU, *I'd Like.*
STEVEN MILLHAUSER, *The Barnum
Museum.*
In the Penny Arcade.
RALPH J. MILLS, JR., *Essays on Poetry.*
MOMUS, *The Book of Jokes.*
CHRISTINE MONTALBETTI, *The Origin
of Man.*
Western.

NICHOLAS MOSLEY, *Accident.*
Assassins.
Catastrophe Practice.
A Garden of Trees.
Hopeful Monsters.
Imago Bird.
Inventing God.
Look at the Dark.
Metamorphosis.
Natalie Natalia.
Serpent.

WARREN MOTTE, *Fables of the Novel:*
French Fiction since 1990.
Fiction Now: The French Novel in the
21st Century.
Mirror Gazing.
Oulipo: A Primer of Potential Literature.

GERALD MURNANE, *Barley Patch.*
Inland.

YVES NAVARRE, *Our Share of Time.*
Sweet Tooth.

DOROTHY NELSON, *In Night's City.*
Tar and Feathers.

ESHKOL NEVO, *Homesick.*

WILFRIDO D. NOLLEDO, *But for*
the Lovers.

BORIS A. NOVAK, *The Master of*
Insomnia.

FLANN O'BRIEN, *At Swim-Two-Birds.*
The Best of Myles.
The Dalkey Archive.
The Hard Life.
The Poor Mouth.
The Third Policeman.

CLAUDE OLLIER, *The Mise-en-Scène.*
Wert and the Life Without End.

PATRIK OUŘEDNÍK, *Europeana.*
The Opportune Moment, 1855.

BORIS PAHOR, *Necropolis.*

FERNANDO DEL PASO, *News from*
the Empire.
Palinuro of Mexico.

ROBERT PINGET, *The Inquisitory.*
Mahu or The Material.
Trio.

MANUEL PUIG, *Betrayed by Rita*
Hayworth.

The Buenos Aires Affair.
Heartbreak Tango.

RAYMOND QUENEAU, *The Last Days.*
Odile.
Pierrot Mon Ami.
Saint Glinglin.

ANN QUIN, *Berg.*
Passages.
Three.
Tripticks.

ISHMAEL REED, *The Free-Lance*
Pallbearers.
The Last Days of Louisiana Red.
Ishmael Reed: The Plays.
Juice!
The Terrible Threes.
The Terrible Twos.
Yellow Back Radio Broke-Down.

JASIA REICHARDT, *15 Journeys Warsaw*
to London.

JOÃO UBALDO RIBEIRO, *House of the*
Fortunate Buddhas.

JEAN RICARDOU, *Place Names.*

RAINER MARIA RILKE,
The Notebooks of Malte Laurids Brigge.

JULIÁN RÍOS, *The House of Ulysses.*
Larva: A Midsummer Night's Babel.
Poundemonium.

ALAIN ROBBE-GRILLET, *Project for a*
Revolution in New York.
A Sentimental Novel.

AUGUSTO ROA BASTOS, *I the Supreme.*

DANIËL ROBBERECHTS, *Arriving in*
Avignon.

JEAN ROLIN, *The Explosion of the*
Radiator Hose.

OLIVIER ROLIN, *Hotel Crystal.*

ALIX CLEO ROUBAUD, *Alix's Journal.*

JACQUES ROUBAUD, *The Form of*
a City Changes Faster, Alas, Than the
Human Heart.
The Great Fire of London.
Hortense in Exile.
Hortense Is Abducted.
Mathematics: The Plurality of Worlds of
Lewis.
Some Thing Black.

RAYMOND ROUSSEL, *Impressions of Africa.*

VEDRANA RUDAN, *Night.*

PABLO M. RUIZ, *Four Cold Chapters on the Possibility of Literature.*

GERMAN SADULAEV, *The Maya Pill.*

TOMAŽ ŠALAMUN, *Soy Realidad.*

LYDIE SALVAYRE, *The Company of Ghosts.*
The Lecture.
The Power of Flies.

LUIS RAFAEL SÁNCHEZ, *Macho Camacho's Beat.*

SEVERO SARDUY, *Cobra & Maitreya.*

NATHALIE SARRAUTE, *Do You Hear Them?*
Martereau.
The Planetarium.

STIG SÆTERBAKKEN, *Siamese.*
Self-Control.
Through the Night.

ARNO SCHMIDT, *Collected Novellas.*
Collected Stories.
Nobodaddy's Children.
Two Novels.

ASAF SCHURR, *Motti.*

GAIL SCOTT, *My Paris.*

DAMION SEARLS, *What We Were Doing and Where We Were Going.*

JUNE AKERS SEESE, *Is This What Other Women Feel Too?*

BERNARD SHARE, *Inish.*
Transit.

VIKTOR SHKLOVSKY, *Bowstring.*
Literature and Cinematography.
Theory of Prose.
Third Factory.
Zoo, or Letters Not about Love.

PIERRE SINIAC, *The Collaborators.*

KJERSTI A. SKOMSVOLD, *The Faster I Walk, the Smaller I Am.*

JOSEF ŠKVORECKÝ, *The Engineer of Human Souls.*

GILBERT SORRENTINO, *Aberration of Starlight.*
Blue Pastoral.
Crystal Vision.

Imaginative Qualities of Actual Things.
Mulligan Stew. Red the Fiend.
Steelwork.
Under the Shadow.

MARKO SOSIČ, *Ballerina, Ballerina.*

ANDRZEJ STASIUK, *Dukla.*
Fado.

GERTRUDE STEIN, *The Making of Americans.*
A Novel of Thank You.

LARS SVENDSEN, *A Philosophy of Evil.*

PIOTR SZEWC, *Annihilation.*

GONÇALO M. TAVARES, *A Man: Klaus Klump.*
Jerusalem.
Learning to Pray in the Age of Technique.

LUCIAN DAN TEODOROVICI, *Our Circus Presents...*

NIKANOR TERATOLOGEN, *Assisted Living.*

STEFAN THEMERSON, *Hobson's Island.*
The Mystery of the Sardine.
Tom Harris.

TAEKO TOMIOKA, *Building Waves.*

JOHN TOOMEY, *Sleepwalker.*

DUMITRU TSEPENEAG, *Hotel Europa.*
The Necessary Marriage.
Pigeon Post.
Vain Art of the Fugue.

ESTHER TUSQUETS, *Stranded.*

DUBRAVKA UGRESIC, *Lend Me Your Character.*
Thank You for Not Reading.

TOR ULVEN, *Replacement.*

MATI UNT, *Brecht at Night.*
Diary of a Blood Donor.
Things in the Night.

ÁLVARO URIBE & OLIVIA SEARS, EDS., *Best of Contemporary Mexican Fiction.*

ELOY URROZ, *Friction.*
The Obstacles.

LUISA VALENZUELA, *Dark Desires and the Others.*
He Who Searches.

PAUL VERHAEGHEN, *Omega Minor.*

BORIS VIAN, *Heartsnatcher.*